Streams of Hope

Christian fiction, Volume 3

Gregory Allen Parker

Published by Graywolf Press, 2024.

This is a work of fiction. Similarities to real people, places, or events are entirely coincidental.

STREAMS OF HOPE

First edition. August 5, 2024.

ISBN: 979-8227878014

Written by Gregory Allen Parker.

Table of Contents

To those who seek hope in the midst of trials,

To the steadfast souls who hold onto faith despite the storms,

And to the beloved memory of my parents, whose unwavering belief
in God's promises inspired this journey.

May these stories light your path and fill your hearts with the eternal
hope that faith provides.

With gratitude and love,

Gregory Allen Parker

Chapter 1: The Prodigal Daughter

A Journey Home

Bible Verse: Luke 15:24 - "For this son of mine was dead and is alive again; he was lost and is found."

1. The Early Years

In the quaint town of Willow Springs, nestled between rolling hills and whispering forests, lived the Thompson family. Among them was Claire Thompson, the youngest daughter, known for her radiant smile and curious spirit. Her early years were filled with the warmth of family love and the guiding principles of faith. The Thompsons were devout Christians, attending Sunday services without fail, their lives centered around the teachings of the Bible.

Claire, with her inquisitive mind, often found herself pondering the stories and lessons shared during the sermons. She loved the parables, especially the one about the prodigal son. Little did she know that one day, her life would mirror that very story.

As Claire grew older, the world beyond Willow Springs began to call to her. The small-town life, once comforting, now felt confining. The allure of the unknown and the promise of freedom beckoned her away from the familiar embrace of her family's faith.

2. The Rebellion

By the time she reached high school, Claire's restlessness had grown into rebellion. She started questioning the beliefs she had been raised with, seeking answers outside the church. Her friends, a mix of the curious and the rebellious, introduced her to a lifestyle far removed from her family's values. Parties, late nights, and risky behavior became the norm.

Her parents, Martha and John Thompson, watched helplessly as their once sweet and obedient daughter slipped away from them. They prayed fervently, hoping for a miracle, but Claire seemed determined to carve out her own path, regardless of the consequences.

The final straw came when Claire announced she was moving to the city for college. Despite their misgivings, her parents supported her decision, hoping the change of environment would help her find herself. Claire saw it as her chance to break free from the past and create a new identity.

3. The City Life

The bustling city of Raleigh was a stark contrast to the quiet charm of Willow Springs. Skyscrapers replaced the rolling hills, and the constant hum of activity drowned out the whispering forests. Claire was exhilarated by the chaos, the endless opportunities, and the anonymity the city offered.

She enrolled in a liberal arts college, majoring in psychology with a minor in philosophy. Her classes exposed her to new ideas and perspectives, further fueling her skepticism towards her upbringing. She immersed herself in the city's nightlife, making new friends who shared her disdain for traditional values.

However, the freedom she sought came at a cost. The excitement of her new life gradually gave way to a sense of emptiness. The parties and late nights that once thrilled her began to feel hollow. The friendships she formed were superficial, based on mutual rebellion rather than genuine connection.

Claire's academic performance started to suffer, and she found herself skipping classes and missing deadlines. Her once vibrant spirit became dull, and she began to question if the life she had chosen was truly what she wanted.

4. The Fall

One fateful night, Claire attended a party that would change her life forever. The music was loud, the lights were blinding, and the air was thick with the scent of alcohol and smoke. Claire, already feeling out of sorts, drank more than usual, trying to drown her growing sense of despair.

As the night wore on, she found herself in a dangerous situation. A group of strangers, sensing her vulnerability, led her away from the safety of her friends.

What followed was a blur of fear, confusion, and regret. Claire's world shattered in that moment, leaving her broken and lost.

In the days that followed, she struggled to come to terms with what had happened. She felt violated, ashamed, and alone. Her friends offered little support, unable or unwilling to understand her pain. Claire's grades plummeted further, and she eventually dropped out of college.

With nowhere else to turn, she reluctantly called her parents. The moment she heard her mother's voice, the dam broke, and she sobbed uncontrollably. Her parents, hearts heavy with grief, welcomed her back home, hoping to help her heal from the trauma she had endured.

5. The Return

Returning to Willow Springs was both a relief and a challenge for Claire. The familiarity of her childhood home brought comfort, but it also reminded her of the innocence she had lost. Her parents, though overjoyed to have her back, struggled to navigate the delicate balance between supporting her and giving her space to heal.

Claire spent her days in a daze, haunted by memories of that fateful night and the choices that led her there. She avoided church, unable to face the judgment she feared from the community. Her parents continued to pray, their faith unwavering, hoping that Claire would find her way back to God.

One Sunday morning, after months of isolation, Claire felt a strange compulsion to attend church. She dressed in her old Sunday best, the fabric feeling foreign against her skin. As she entered the familiar sanctuary, she was greeted by warm smiles and gentle nods. The congregation, aware of her struggles, welcomed her without judgment.

The sermon that day was about forgiveness and redemption. The pastor spoke of God's unwavering love and the story of the prodigal son. Claire felt a surge of emotion as she listened, her heart aching with the weight of her sins and the possibility of redemption.

6. The Turning Point

That afternoon, Claire found herself alone in her room, the words of the sermon echoing in her mind. She picked up her Bible, its pages worn from years of neglect, and turned to the story of the prodigal son. As she read, tears streamed down her face. She saw herself in the wayward son, lost and broken, but still loved by the father.

Claire fell to her knees, her heart heavy with guilt and regret. She prayed for the first time in years, asking God for forgiveness and guidance. She poured out her pain, her fears, and her hopes, feeling a sense of peace she hadn't known in a long time.

Her parents, sensing a change in their daughter, continued to support her with love and patience. They encouraged her to seek counseling, both professional and spiritual, to help her heal from her trauma. Claire reluctantly agreed, understanding that she couldn't do it alone.

7. The Healing Process

Claire's journey to healing was slow and arduous. Her counselor, a kind and empathetic woman named Sarah, helped her navigate the complex emotions she was experiencing. They discussed the trauma she had endured, the choices she had made, and the underlying issues that had led her astray.

Through counseling, Claire began to understand the importance of forgiveness, not just from others, but from herself. She grappled with her guilt and shame, learning to let go of the past and focus on the present. Her faith, once a distant memory, became a source of strength and comfort.

She also reconnected with the church community, attending Bible study groups and volunteering in various church activities. The support and understanding she received from the congregation helped her rebuild her self-esteem and sense of purpose.

8. Finding Purpose

As Claire's faith grew stronger, so did her desire to help others who were struggling. She decided to return to college, this time with a clear goal in mind.

She switched her major to social work, inspired by her own journey and the support she had received from her counselor.

Her parents, though initially hesitant, supported her decision wholeheartedly. They saw the fire in her eyes, the determination to turn her life around and make a difference in the world. Claire's grades improved, and she found herself thriving in her new field of study.

Claire's experience in the city had left scars, but it also gave her a unique perspective and empathy for those in similar situations. She volunteered at a local shelter, working with women who had experienced trauma and abuse. Her own story became a source of inspiration and hope for those she helped.

9. Redemption

Years passed, and Claire graduated with honors, her family beaming with pride. She secured a job at a reputable non-profit organization, dedicated to helping survivors of abuse and trauma. Her faith, once lost, had been restored, and she felt a renewed sense of purpose and fulfillment.

Claire's work was challenging but rewarding. She encountered heartbreaking stories and witnessed incredible resilience. Each day, she drew strength from her faith, knowing that God had a plan for her and those she helped.

One day, Claire received a letter from a young woman she had counseled. The woman expressed her gratitude, sharing how Claire's story had given her the courage to rebuild her life. Claire felt a surge of joy and fulfillment, knowing that her journey had made a difference.

10. A New Beginning

Claire's journey of faith and redemption had come full circle. She had faced her demons, found healing, and dedicated her life to helping others. Her relationship with her family had grown stronger, and she had found a new sense of belonging in her church community.

Her past, once a source of shame, had become a testament to God's grace and love. Claire often shared her story, hoping to inspire others to find their way back to faith and redemption. She knew that her journey was far from over, but she was no longer lost. She had been found.

11. Embracing Faith

As Claire continued her work at the non-profit, she felt a deeper calling to share her story and faith with a wider audience. She began speaking at churches, schools, and community centers, telling her story of rebellion, loss, and redemption. Her authenticity and vulnerability touched many hearts, and she became a sought-after speaker.

Her parents, ever supportive, attended her events, beaming with pride as they watched their daughter inspire others. They knew that their prayers had been answered, and they thanked God every day for bringing Claire back to them.

Claire also started a blog, writing about her experiences and the lessons she had learned along the way. Her posts resonated with readers, many of whom reached out to share their own stories of struggle and faith. Claire's online presence grew, and she found herself part of a larger community of believers, united by their shared experiences.

12. Building a Legacy

As Claire's influence grew, she felt a calling to do more. She decided to establish a foundation dedicated to helping young women who had experienced trauma and were seeking a path to healing. The foundation, named "Streams of Hope," aimed to provide counseling, support, and resources to those in need.

With the support of her family, church, and community, Claire launched the foundation. The response was overwhelming, and she was humbled by the generosity and support she received. "Streams of Hope" quickly became a beacon of light for many, offering hope and healing to those who had lost their way.

Claire's foundation also focused on education and prevention, working with schools and communities to raise awareness about the dangers of risky behavior and the importance of faith and support systems. She believed that by addressing these issues early, many young women could avoid the path she had taken.

13. Personal Growth

Through her work with the foundation, Claire continued to grow both personally and spiritually. She deepened her understanding of her faith, studying the Bible and seeking guidance from her pastor and mentors. Her relationship with God became the cornerstone of her life, guiding her decisions and actions.

Claire also found time to nurture her own well-being. She practiced self-care, knowing that she needed to be strong and healthy to help others. She spent time in nature, finding solace and inspiration in the beauty of God's creation. She also maintained close relationships with her family and friends, cherishing the support and love they provided.

14. Love and Family

Amidst her busy life, Claire met a kind and compassionate man named David. They met through a mutual friend at church, and their shared faith and values brought them close. David admired Claire's strength and dedication, and Claire found comfort and joy in his presence.

Their relationship blossomed, and they supported each other through life's challenges. David became an integral part of Claire's life, offering unwavering support for her work with the foundation. They prayed together, attended church together, and dreamed of building a future together.

In time, David proposed, and Claire joyfully accepted. Their wedding was a celebration of love, faith, and the journey they had both undertaken. Surrounded by family and friends, they vowed to walk together in faith, supporting each other in their shared mission of helping others.

15. Continuing the Journey

Claire's story of the prodigal daughter was one of loss, rebellion, and redemption. Her journey had taken her from the depths of despair to the heights of faith and fulfillment. She had found her way back to God, and in doing so, discovered her true purpose in life.

Her work with the foundation continued to thrive, helping countless young women find hope and healing. Claire's speaking engagements and writing inspired many, and her story became a powerful testament to the transformative power of faith.

Claire knew that her journey was far from over. She faced new challenges and opportunities every day, but she embraced them with a sense of peace and purpose. Her faith remained her guiding light, and she trusted that God would continue to lead her on the path He had chosen for her.

As Claire looked back on her life, she felt a deep sense of gratitude. She had been lost, but now she was found. She had been broken, but now she was whole. Her story was a testament to God's grace and love, and she was determined to share that message with the world.

In the end, Claire's journey was not just about her own redemption, but about the countless lives she touched along the way. Her story of faith and hope continued to inspire, reminding everyone that no matter how far they had strayed, they could always find their way back to God.

Conclusion

Claire's story in "Streams of Hope: An Anthology of Faith" serves as a powerful reminder of the transformative power of faith, forgiveness, and love. Her journey from rebellion to redemption, from loss to fulfillment, illustrates the timeless truth of Luke 15:24: "For this son of mine was dead and is alive again; he was lost and is found."

Claire's life became a beacon of hope for those struggling with their own demons, showing them that it is never too late to return to faith and find a renewed sense of purpose. Her foundation, "Streams of Hope," continues to make a difference, offering support and healing to those in need.

Through her story, Claire's message is clear: no matter how far you have strayed, God's love is always there, ready to welcome you home.

Chapter 2: Faith in the Storm

Bible Verse: Psalm 46:1 - "God is our refuge and strength, an ever-present help in trouble."

1. The Calm Before the Storm

The Jenkins family lived in the coastal town of Seaview, a picturesque community known for its serene beaches and friendly neighbors. Henry and Laura Jenkins had built a comfortable life with their two children, Emily and Jack. They were a close-knit family, bound by love and faith, and were active members of their local church.

Seaview had always been a haven for the Jenkins family, a place where they found peace and solace. They loved their home, a cozy cottage nestled a few blocks from the beach, where they often enjoyed family picnics and evening walks along the shore. Life was idyllic, filled with laughter, love, and a deep sense of belonging.

However, the tranquility of their lives was about to be shattered by an unexpected force of nature.

2. The Warning

It was a typical sunny afternoon when the first warning came. Henry was at work, Laura was tending to her garden, and the children were playing in the yard. The local news station interrupted its regular programming to announce that a powerful hurricane was forming in the Atlantic and heading toward their region.

At first, the Jenkins family, like many others in Seaview, didn't take the warning too seriously. Hurricanes were not uncommon, and they had weathered several storms over the years without significant damage. But as the hours passed, the reports grew more urgent, and the projected path of the hurricane became increasingly concerning.

Henry and Laura gathered the children inside and turned on the news. The meteorologist spoke in grave tones about the potential strength of the hurricane, urging residents to prepare for the worst. The governor declared a state of emergency, and evacuation orders were issued for coastal areas.

The Jenkins family knew they had to act quickly. Henry and Laura made a list of essentials, and they began to gather supplies. They filled their car with water, non-perishable food, important documents, and family mementos. Emily and Jack, though frightened, helped as best they could, sensing the gravity of the situation.

3. The Evacuation

By evening, the streets of Seaview were filled with the sounds of sirens and the sight of families packing up and leaving their homes. The Jenkins family loaded their car and said a prayer before heading to the community shelter located inland. The drive was tense, with traffic moving slowly as thousands of residents fled the impending storm.

At the shelter, they were greeted by volunteers who provided blankets, food, and water. The large gymnasium had been converted into a temporary refuge, with cots lined up in rows and families huddled together, sharing their fears and hopes.

As the night wore on, the winds outside grew stronger, and the rain began to fall in sheets. The sound of the storm was deafening, a constant reminder of the power and unpredictability of nature. Henry and Laura did their best to comfort Emily and Jack, assuring them that they were safe and that they would get through this together.

In the midst of the chaos, the family found solace in their faith. They joined hands and prayed, seeking strength and protection from God. Their prayers brought a sense of calm, a reminder that they were not alone in their struggle.

4. The Storm

The hurricane made landfall in the early hours of the morning, unleashing its fury on the coastal towns. Seaview bore the brunt of the storm, with winds exceeding 150 miles per hour and storm surges flooding the streets. Trees were uprooted, buildings were damaged, and power lines were downed, plunging the town into darkness.

At the shelter, the families listened in fear as the storm raged outside. The walls shook, and the roof creaked under the pressure of the wind. Volunteers moved through the rows of cots, offering words of encouragement and checking on the well-being of the evacuees.

Henry and Laura held their children close, whispering reassurances and praying for the safety of their home and community. They knew that the storm would pass, but the uncertainty of what they would find in its aftermath weighed heavily on their minds.

As dawn broke, the winds began to subside, and the rain lessened to a steady drizzle. The storm had passed, leaving behind a trail of destruction. The residents of the shelter slowly emerged, anxious to return to their homes and assess the damage.

5. The Aftermath

The drive back to Seaview was somber, with scenes of devastation greeting them at every turn. Fallen trees blocked the roads, debris was scattered everywhere, and homes were damaged or destroyed. The once-beautiful town was now a landscape of chaos and ruin.

When the Jenkins family arrived at their street, their hearts sank. Their beloved cottage had suffered significant damage. The roof had partially collapsed, windows were shattered, and water had flooded the lower level. It was a heartbreaking sight, but they were grateful to be safe and together.

Neighbors emerged from their homes, dazed and distraught. The community came together, helping each other clear debris and check on the well-being of their friends and family. Despite the destruction, there was a sense of unity and resilience, a determination to rebuild and recover.

Henry and Laura led their children in a prayer of gratitude for their safety and a plea for strength in the days ahead. They knew that their faith would be crucial in helping them navigate the challenges they now faced.

6. Rebuilding

The days and weeks that followed were a blur of activity and emotion. The Jenkins family focused on cleaning up the debris and making their home habitable again. Volunteers from their church and community offered assistance, providing food, supplies, and manpower.

Henry took time off work to help with the repairs, while Laura coordinated with insurance adjusters and contractors. Emily and Jack, though young, contributed in their own ways, helping to sort through belongings and offering moral support.

Throughout the rebuilding process, the family's faith remained a source of strength. They attended church services regularly, finding comfort in the familiar hymns and the support of their congregation. The pastor's sermons emphasized hope and resilience, reminding them that God was with them in their struggles.

The Jenkins family also participated in community outreach efforts, helping neighbors who were in even greater need. They volunteered at the local food bank, distributed supplies, and offered a listening ear to those who were grieving the loss of their homes and loved ones.

7. The Power of Faith

As the weeks turned into months, the Jenkins family began to see progress. Their home, though still in need of repairs, was slowly being restored. The community of Seaview showed remarkable resilience, with neighbors supporting each other and working together to rebuild.

Throughout this journey, the family's faith deepened. They experienced firsthand the power of prayer and the strength that comes from trusting in God's plan. They realized that their material possessions, though important, were not the foundation of their lives. Their true strength came from their faith and their love for each other.

Emily and Jack, despite their young age, gained a profound understanding of the importance of faith and community. They saw their parents' unwavering trust in God and the impact it had on their ability to cope with adversity. It was a lesson that would stay with them for the rest of their lives.

8. Renewed Purpose

The storm had taken much from the Jenkins family, but it had also given them a renewed sense of purpose. They became more involved in their church and community, using their experience to help others who were facing similar challenges.

Laura started a support group for families affected by the hurricane, offering a space for them to share their stories and find comfort in each other. The group grew quickly, becoming a vital resource for those in need. Laura's compassion and leadership were a testament to her faith and determination.

Henry, too, found new ways to contribute. He joined a disaster response team organized by their church, traveling to other affected areas to assist with rebuilding efforts. His skills and experience were invaluable, and he found fulfillment in helping others recover from their own storms.

Emily and Jack continued to thrive, drawing strength from their family's faith and the support of their community. They participated in church activities and volunteered alongside their parents, learning the importance of service and compassion.

9. A Community United

The hurricane had left a lasting mark on Seaview, but it also brought the community closer together. Neighbors who had once been strangers now worked side by side, united by a common goal of rebuilding their town and supporting each other.

The church played a central role in this effort, organizing relief efforts, providing spiritual guidance, and fostering a sense of unity. The Jenkins family, inspired by their own journey, became leaders in these efforts, helping to coordinate volunteer activities and support services.

The annual town festival, which had been postponed due to the storm, was rescheduled as a celebration of resilience and hope. The community gathered in the town square, sharing food, music, and stories of survival. It was a joyous occasion, a testament to the strength and spirit of Seaview.

During the festival, the pastor gave a special sermon, reflecting on the challenges they had faced and the power of faith in overcoming adversity. He quoted Psalm 46:1, "God is our refuge and strength, an ever-present help in trouble," reminding everyone that their faith had been a guiding light in the darkest of times.

10. Lessons Learned

The hurricane had taught the Jenkins family many valuable lessons. They had learned the importance of preparedness, the strength of community, and the power of faith. They had faced their fears and losses with courage, emerging stronger and more united.

They also learned to appreciate the simple joys of life. The sound of laughter, the warmth of a hug, the beauty of a sunset – these were the moments that truly mattered. They realized that their faith and love for each other were the foundation of their resilience.

The experience also deepened their empathy for others. They became more aware of the struggles faced by those around them and more committed to offering help and support. Their faith inspired them to be a source of light and hope for others, just as their community had been for them.

11. Moving Forward

As time passed, the scars left by the hurricane began to heal. Homes were rebuilt, businesses reopened, and the community of Seaview thrived once again. The Jenkins family continued their work, both in their personal lives and within their community, always guided by their faith.

Henry returned to work, bringing with him a renewed sense of purpose and gratitude. Laura continued to lead her support group, helping families navigate their own journeys of recovery. Emily and Jack excelled in school, their resilience and faith shining through in everything they did.

The family also made time for each other, cherishing the moments they had together. They took regular walks along the beach, went on family picnics, and attended church services together. Their bond was stronger than ever, fortified by the challenges they had faced and the faith that had guided them through.

12. Reflections

One evening, as the sun set over Seaview, the Jenkins family gathered on their front porch, reflecting on the journey they had undertaken. They talked about the storm, the fear and uncertainty they had felt, and the strength they had found in their faith and each other.

Henry spoke about the importance of trusting in God's plan, even when the path ahead seemed unclear. Laura shared her gratitude for the support of their community and the comfort they had found in their faith. Emily and Jack talked about the lessons they had learned and the ways they hoped to help others in the future.

Together, they prayed, thanking God for His guidance and protection. They knew that their journey was not over, that life would bring new challenges and opportunities. But they were confident in their faith and their ability to face whatever lay ahead, knowing that God was their refuge and strength.

13. A New Chapter

With the hurricane behind them, the Jenkins family embraced a new chapter in their lives. They continued to grow in their faith, finding new ways to serve and support their community. Their experiences had shaped them, deepening their empathy and strengthening their resolve.

The foundation of their lives was not the physical home they had rebuilt, but the faith and love that bound them together. They were a family united by their shared experiences and their trust in God's plan.

As they moved forward, they carried with them the lessons of the storm. They knew that challenges would come, but they also knew that they had the strength and faith to overcome them. Their journey was a testament to the power of faith, the strength of community, and the resilience of the human spirit.

14. Sharing Their Story

The Jenkins family felt a calling to share their story with others. They believed that their journey of faith and resilience could inspire and comfort those facing their own storms. They began speaking at churches, schools, and community events, sharing their experiences and the lessons they had learned.

Their story resonated with many, offering a message of hope and encouragement. They emphasized the importance of faith, the power of community, and the strength that comes from trusting in God's plan. Their authenticity and vulnerability touched many hearts, inspiring others to find strength in their faith and to support those in need.

They also started a blog, documenting their journey and offering resources and support for those facing similar challenges. The blog became a source of inspiration and comfort for many, a testament to the impact of their faith and the power of their story.

15. Legacy of Faith

As the years passed, the Jenkins family's story of faith in the storm became a legacy. Their experiences had shaped them, deepening their faith and strengthening their resolve. They had faced their fears and losses with courage, emerging stronger and more united.

Their faith had been their refuge and strength, guiding them through the darkest of times and helping them rebuild their lives. They had learned the importance of community, the power of compassion, and the resilience of the human spirit.

Their journey was a testament to the enduring power of faith, a reminder that no matter how fierce the storm, God is always with us, offering strength and refuge. The Jenkins family's story of faith in the storm continued to inspire and comfort those facing their own challenges, a legacy of hope and resilience that would endure for generations to come.

Conclusion

The Jenkins family's story in "Streams of Hope: An Anthology of Faith" serves as a powerful reminder of the strength and resilience that comes from faith. Their journey through the storm, their unwavering trust in God's plan, and their commitment to helping others illustrate the timeless truth of Psalm 46:1: "God is our refuge and strength, an ever-present help in trouble."

Their story is a testament to the power of faith to overcome fear and loss, to the strength of community in times of adversity, and to the enduring resilience of the human spirit. The Jenkins family's legacy of faith in the storm continues to inspire and comfort, reminding us all that no matter how fierce the storm, we are never alone.

Chapter 3: Healing Hands

Bible Verse: James 5:15 - "And the prayer offered in faith will make the sick person well; the Lord will raise them up."

1. The Beginning

Dr. Samuel Harris had always believed in the power of medicine. From a young age, he was fascinated by the human body and the ability of science to heal. He pursued his medical degree with passion, graduating at the top of his class and quickly establishing himself as a talented and dedicated physician.

Samuel's faith in science was strong, but his faith in God was more complex. Raised in a devout Christian family, he had grown distant from his religious roots during his years of medical training. The demands of his profession left little time for church or prayer, and he often found himself questioning the existence of a higher power in the face of suffering and illness.

His wife, Rachel, was a source of spiritual strength in their family. She was a nurse and a devout Christian, her faith unwavering despite the challenges they faced in their professional lives. Rachel often encouraged Samuel to join her in prayer, but he remained skeptical, believing that medicine alone held the answers.

2. The Patient

One rainy evening, Samuel received an urgent call from the hospital. A critically ill patient had been admitted, and the situation was dire. He rushed to the emergency room, his mind focused on the medical challenges ahead.

The patient was a young woman named Emily Carter. She had been involved in a severe car accident and had sustained multiple life-threatening injuries. Her condition was critical, and the prognosis was grim. The medical team worked tirelessly to stabilize her, but the odds were against them.

As Samuel reviewed her medical charts and scans, he felt a sense of helplessness. Despite their best efforts, Emily's condition continued to deteriorate. Her vital signs were unstable, and she showed no signs of improvement. The situation was dire, and the medical team began to prepare for the worst.

Emily's parents, Mark and Susan Carter, arrived at the hospital, their faces etched with worry and fear. They were devout Christians and immediately began to pray for their daughter's recovery. Samuel watched as they held each other's hands, their faith providing them with a sense of hope and strength.

3. The Struggle

Days turned into weeks, and Emily remained in critical condition. The medical team exhausted every option, but her body showed no signs of responding to treatment. Samuel felt a growing sense of frustration and helplessness. He had dedicated his life to healing, but in this case, his skills seemed insufficient.

Rachel, aware of the toll the situation was taking on her husband, encouraged him to take a break and join her in prayer. "Samuel," she said gently, "sometimes we need to seek help beyond what we can see and understand. Prayer can bring comfort and strength, even in the darkest of times."

Reluctantly, Samuel agreed to pray with Rachel. They knelt by their bed and prayed for Emily's recovery, asking God for guidance and strength. It was a moment of vulnerability for Samuel, a step outside his comfort zone, but he found a strange sense of peace in the act of prayer.

The next day, Samuel returned to the hospital, feeling a renewed sense of determination. He was greeted by Mark and Susan, who shared with him their unwavering faith that Emily would recover. They spoke of the power of prayer and the miracles they believed were possible through God's intervention.

4. A Glimmer of Hope

One morning, as Samuel was making his rounds, he noticed a slight improvement in Emily's condition. Her vital signs were more stable, and there were subtle signs of healing. It was a small but significant change, and it filled him with cautious optimism.

He shared the news with Mark and Susan, who responded with gratitude and renewed hope. "We believe that God's hand is at work," Susan said with tears in her eyes. "We have been praying day and night, and we trust that He will heal our daughter."

Samuel, though still skeptical, couldn't deny the possibility that something beyond medicine was at play. He continued to monitor Emily closely, adjusting her treatment as needed, but he also found himself praying for her recovery. It was a strange and unfamiliar territory for him, blending his medical expertise with a newfound sense of faith.

5. The Turning Point

As the days passed, Emily's condition continued to improve. Her wounds began to heal, and she showed signs of regaining consciousness. The medical team was astonished by her progress, considering the severity of her injuries. It was a turnaround that seemed almost miraculous.

One evening, as Samuel was preparing to leave the hospital, he was approached by Mark and Susan. They had brought their pastor, Reverend James, to visit Emily and offer prayers for her continued recovery. Reverend James was a kind and compassionate man, his presence exuding a sense of calm and reassurance.

"Dr. Harris," Reverend James said, "I would like to pray for Emily, and I would be honored if you would join us."

Samuel hesitated for a moment, but then nodded in agreement. They gathered around Emily's bedside, holding hands and bowing their heads. Reverend James led the prayer, his words filled with faith and hope, asking for God's healing touch to be upon Emily.

As they prayed, Samuel felt a profound sense of connection and peace. He realized that prayer was not just about asking for miracles, but about finding strength and solace in the face of uncertainty. It was a way to surrender control and trust in something greater than oneself.

6. The Miracle

Emily's recovery continued at an astonishing pace. Within a few weeks, she regained consciousness and began to communicate with her family and medical team. Her wounds healed, and she gradually regained her strength. It was a recovery that defied medical explanations, a true miracle in the eyes of those who witnessed it.

Samuel was deeply moved by Emily's recovery. He had witnessed countless cases in his career, but this one was different. It had challenged his beliefs and opened his heart to the possibility of divine intervention. He couldn't deny the power of prayer and the role it had played in Emily's healing.

Mark and Susan were overjoyed, their faith reaffirmed by their daughter's miraculous recovery. They expressed their gratitude to Samuel and the medical team, but they also credited their prayers and God's grace for the miracle they had witnessed.

Emily's case became a source of inspiration for the entire hospital. Her story was shared among patients and staff, a testament to the power of faith and the resilience of the human spirit. It was a reminder that, even in the face of overwhelming odds, there was always hope.

7. A New Perspective

Samuel's experience with Emily profoundly impacted his perspective on medicine and faith. He began to see prayer and spirituality as complementary to medical treatment, rather than separate or contradictory. He realized that healing was not just about the body, but also about the mind and spirit.

He started to incorporate prayer and spiritual support into his practice, offering to pray with patients and their families if they desired. He found that it brought comfort and reassurance to many, helping them cope with their illnesses and find strength in their faith.

Samuel also deepened his own spiritual journey. He began attending church with Rachel regularly, finding solace and inspiration in the sermons and community. His relationship with God grew stronger, and he found a sense of peace and purpose that he had not known before.

8. Emily's Gratitude

Emily's recovery was nothing short of miraculous, and she was filled with gratitude for the second chance at life she had been given. She often reflected on the prayers and support she had received from her family, friends, and the medical team.

One day, as she was preparing to leave the hospital, she asked to speak with Samuel. "Dr. Harris," she said, her voice filled with emotion, "I want to thank you for everything you've done for me. Your skill and dedication saved my life, but I also believe that the prayers and faith of my family played a crucial role in my recovery."

Samuel smiled, humbled by her words. "Emily, your strength and resilience have been remarkable. I am honored to have been a part of your journey, and I have also learned a great deal from this experience. Your faith has inspired me, and I believe that it played a significant role in your healing."

Emily nodded, tears in her eyes. "I will never forget the prayers and support I received. It has changed my life in ways I cannot fully express. I am determined to live my life with purpose and to share the power of faith with others."

9. A New Chapter

As Emily left the hospital and began her journey of recovery at home, she dedicated herself to helping others who were facing similar challenges. She became an advocate for the power of prayer and faith in healing, sharing her story with churches, support groups, and community organizations.

She also pursued a career in healthcare, inspired by the dedication and compassion of the medical team that had cared for her. Emily's experience had ignited a passion within her to make a difference in the lives of others, to offer hope and healing to those in need.

Samuel continued to practice medicine with a renewed sense of purpose and faith. He built strong relationships with his patients, offering not only medical expertise but also spiritual support. He found that his patients responded positively, experiencing not only physical healing but also emotional and spiritual growth.

10. The Power of Faith

The story of Emily's miraculous recovery spread throughout the community, inspiring many to explore the power of faith in their own lives. The local church saw an increase in attendance, with many seeking spiritual guidance and support.

Reverend James often shared Emily's story in his sermons, emphasizing the importance of prayer and faith in overcoming adversity. He encouraged the congregation to trust in God's plan and to seek His guidance in times of need.

Mark and Susan continued to be active members of the church, their faith strengthened by the miracle they had witnessed. They often shared their testimony, offering encouragement and hope to others facing difficult circumstances.

11. Samuel's Journey

Samuel's journey of faith and medicine was ongoing. He continued to learn and grow, both as a physician and as a believer. He attended conferences on spirituality and healthcare, exploring ways to integrate faith into his practice.

He also began writing about his experiences, sharing his insights and reflections in medical journals and spiritual publications. His articles sparked discussions and debates, challenging others in the medical field to consider the role of faith in healing.

Samuel's relationship with Rachel grew stronger as they shared their faith journey together. They prayed together, attended church together, and supported each other in their professional and personal lives. Their love and faith were intertwined, providing a strong foundation for their family.

12. Community Impact

The impact of Emily's recovery and Samuel's journey extended beyond the hospital and the church. The community of Seaview was inspired by their story, finding renewed hope and strength in their own lives.

Local organizations began to offer support groups and resources for those seeking spiritual and emotional healing. The hospital implemented programs to provide spiritual care for patients and their families, recognizing the importance of addressing the whole person.

The power of faith and prayer became a central theme in the community, fostering a sense of unity and compassion. People came together to support each other, sharing their stories and offering encouragement and prayer.

13. A Continuing Legacy

As the years passed, the legacy of Emily's miraculous recovery and Samuel's journey of faith continued to grow. Their story was shared in books, articles, and documentaries, reaching a wider audience and inspiring many to explore the power of faith in their own lives.

Emily's advocacy work and healthcare career flourished, making a significant impact on the lives of those she touched. She continued to share her testimony, offering hope and healing to those in need.

Samuel's practice thrived, and he became a respected leader in the integration of faith and medicine. His work influenced many in the medical field, encouraging a more holistic approach to healthcare that addressed the physical, emotional, and spiritual needs of patients.

14. Reflections

One evening, as Samuel and Rachel sat on their porch, they reflected on the journey they had undertaken. They talked about the challenges they had faced, the lessons they had learned, and the impact their faith had on their lives and the lives of others.

Samuel spoke about the transformation he had experienced, both as a physician and as a believer. "Rachel, I am grateful for your unwavering faith and for encouraging me to explore the power of prayer. It has changed my life in ways I never imagined."

Rachel smiled, her eyes filled with love and pride. "Samuel, I always knew that you had a compassionate heart and a desire to help others. Your journey has been an inspiration to me and to so many others. I am grateful to walk this path with you."

They prayed together, thanking God for His guidance and for the miracles they had witnessed. They knew that their journey was ongoing, that there were still challenges and opportunities ahead. But they faced the future with confidence, trusting in God's plan and the power of faith.

15. A Testament of Faith

The story of Emily's miraculous recovery and Samuel's journey of faith became a testament to the power of prayer and the resilience of the human spirit. It was a reminder that healing was not just about the body, but also about the mind and spirit.

Their journey illustrated the timeless truth of James 5:15: "And the prayer offered in faith will make the sick person well; the Lord will raise them up." It was a testament to the strength and comfort that faith could provide in times of uncertainty and suffering.

As their story continued to inspire and comfort those facing their own challenges, it served as a beacon of hope and a reminder that, even in the darkest of times, there was always a source of strength and healing to be found in faith.

Conclusion

The chapter "Healing Hands" in "Streams of Hope: An Anthology of Faith" tells the remarkable story of a doctor's journey of faith and the miraculous recovery of a critically ill patient. It illustrates the power of prayer and the importance of addressing the whole person—body, mind, and spirit—in the healing process.

Dr. Samuel Harris's transformation from a skeptical physician to a believer in the power of prayer is a powerful testament to the impact of faith on healing. Emily's recovery serves as a source of inspiration and hope, reminding us all that, even in the face of overwhelming odds, there is always hope and strength to be found in faith.

Their story, grounded in the biblical verse James 5:15, "And the prayer offered in faith will make the sick person well; the Lord will raise them up," is a testament to the enduring power of faith and the resilience of the human spirit. It continues to inspire and comfort those facing their own challenges, offering a message of hope and healing that transcends the boundaries of medicine and science.

Chapter 4: The Shepherd's Voice

Bible Verse: John 10:27 - "My sheep listen to my voice; I know them, and they follow me."

1. The Fall

Mark Stevens had always been a man of ambition. Growing up in a small town, he dreamed of escaping to the big city and making a name for himself. He worked hard in school, earning scholarships and accolades, and eventually landed a job at a prestigious law firm in the heart of New York City.

For years, Mark's life seemed perfect. He climbed the corporate ladder, enjoying the perks of success: a high salary, a luxury apartment, and a network of influential friends. But beneath the surface, Mark was struggling. The relentless pressure of his job, coupled with the isolation of city life, left him feeling empty and disillusioned.

Mark's descent began subtly. He started drinking more, seeking solace in alcohol to numb the stress and loneliness. His performance at work began to suffer, and he found himself making mistakes that he never would have made in his earlier, more focused years. His relationships with friends and family deteriorated as he pushed them away, preferring solitude over the risk of vulnerability.

One particularly bad day at work, Mark was reprimanded by his boss for a costly error. Feeling humiliated and defeated, he left the office early and went straight to a bar. As he drowned his sorrows in whiskey, he couldn't shake the feeling that his life was spiraling out of control.

2. The Turning Point

That evening, Mark decided to take a walk to clear his mind. The city streets, usually bustling with energy, felt oppressive and suffocating. He wandered aimlessly, his thoughts a chaotic mix of regret and despair.

As he walked, he found himself in front of a small, unassuming church. The door was open, and a warm light spilled out onto the sidewalk. Feeling drawn to the light, Mark hesitated for a moment before stepping inside.

The church was empty, save for a few flickering candles and the faint sound of a choir practicing in the distance. Mark sat down in a pew, the quiet and calm of the sanctuary offering a stark contrast to the chaos of his mind. He closed his eyes and took a deep breath, feeling a sense of peace that he hadn't felt in years.

After a few moments, Mark opened his eyes and noticed a figure approaching him. It was a middle-aged man with kind eyes and a gentle smile. He introduced himself as Pastor John and asked if Mark needed someone to talk to.

3. The Shepherd's Voice

Mark was hesitant at first, unsure of what to say. But there was something about Pastor John's presence that made him feel safe. He began to open up, sharing his struggles and fears, the weight of his regrets and the emptiness he felt inside.

Pastor John listened patiently, offering no judgment or advice, just a compassionate ear. When Mark finished, Pastor John spoke softly, sharing words of comfort and hope. He talked about the love and grace of God, and how even in the darkest moments, there was always a path to redemption.

"God knows you, Mark," Pastor John said, his voice filled with conviction. "He knows your struggles and your pain, and He is always with you, even when you feel lost. You are His sheep, and He is your Shepherd. Listen to His voice, and He will guide you."

Mark was deeply moved by Pastor John's words. For the first time in a long time, he felt a glimmer of hope. He realized that he had been trying to navigate his life on his own, without seeking guidance or support. The idea of a loving Shepherd who knew him and cared for him was both comforting and transformative.

4. A New Beginning

In the days that followed, Mark found himself returning to the church. He attended services, listened to Pastor John's sermons, and began to reconnect with his faith. The teachings of the Bible, which he had dismissed as irrelevant in his pursuit of success, now resonated deeply with him.

Mark also began meeting with Pastor John regularly. They talked about faith, life, and the struggles that Mark faced. Pastor John became a mentor and friend, guiding Mark with wisdom and compassion. He encouraged Mark to find healthy ways to cope with stress, to rebuild his relationships, and to seek a balanced and fulfilling life.

One evening, as they sat in Pastor John's office, Mark shared his fears about the future. "I've made so many mistakes," he said, his voice filled with regret. "I'm not sure I can turn my life around."

Pastor John smiled gently. "Mark, God's grace is boundless. He forgives our mistakes and offers us a chance to start anew. It's never too late to change your path. Trust in Him, and He will lead you."

5. Rebuilding Relationships

Mark took Pastor John's words to heart. He reached out to his family, apologizing for pushing them away and seeking to rebuild their relationships. His parents and siblings were initially wary, but they could see the sincerity in Mark's efforts and welcomed him back with open arms.

Reconnecting with his family brought a sense of belonging and support that Mark had been missing. He spent time with his parents, enjoying long conversations and family meals. He reestablished connections with his siblings, sharing in their joys and challenges.

Mark also reached out to old friends, those he had lost touch with during his pursuit of success. Some relationships were beyond repair, but others were rekindled, and Mark found comfort in the renewed bonds of friendship.

6. Finding Balance

One of the biggest challenges Mark faced was finding balance in his life. He realized that his all-consuming pursuit of career success had left little room for anything else. With Pastor John's guidance, Mark began to make changes.

He reduced his hours at work, prioritizing his well-being and personal life. He found new hobbies and interests, exploring activities that brought him joy and fulfillment. He started volunteering at the church, helping with community outreach programs and finding a sense of purpose in serving others.

Mark also sought professional help to address his struggles with alcohol and stress. With the support of a therapist, he learned healthier coping mechanisms and strategies for managing his anxiety. The process was challenging, but Mark was determined to build a better, more balanced life.

7. The Power of Prayer

Throughout his journey, prayer became an integral part of Mark's life. He found solace in speaking to God, sharing his hopes, fears, and gratitude. Prayer became a source of strength, a way to connect with his faith and seek guidance.

One evening, as Mark knelt by his bed, he felt a deep sense of peace. He had been reflecting on his journey, the transformation he had experienced, and the people who had supported him along the way. He thanked God for His grace and asked for continued guidance in his life.

As he prayed, Mark remembered Pastor John's words: "My sheep listen to my voice; I know them, and they follow me." He realized that he had been listening to the Shepherd's voice, trusting in God's plan, and following His guidance.

8. A Test of Faith

Mark's newfound sense of direction and balance was put to the test when he faced a difficult situation at work. A high-stakes case, with significant implications for the firm and its clients, required his attention. The pressure was immense, and Mark felt the familiar weight of stress and anxiety.

In the past, Mark would have turned to alcohol to cope, but he now had healthier strategies and a strong support system. He sought guidance from Pastor John, who reminded him to trust in God's plan and to find strength in prayer.

Mark also relied on his family and friends, sharing his struggles and seeking their encouragement. Their support reminded him that he was not alone, and that he had people who cared for him and believed in him.

Through prayer and determination, Mark navigated the challenging case, relying on his skills and the support of his colleagues. The experience was difficult, but it reinforced his commitment to a balanced and faith-centered life.

9. The Shepherd's Voice

As Mark's life continued to transform, he often reflected on the moment he had walked into the church and met Pastor John. That chance encounter had set him on a path of healing and growth, guided by the Shepherd's voice.

Mark realized that the Shepherd's voice was not always loud or obvious. It was often a gentle whisper, a sense of peace, or a feeling of direction. Listening to the Shepherd's voice required faith, trust, and the willingness to follow, even when the path was unclear.

One Sunday, during a church service, Pastor John spoke about the parable of the lost sheep. He emphasized that God seeks out the lost and rejoices when they are found. Mark felt a deep connection to the message, knowing that he had been one of the lost sheep, now found and embraced by God's love.

10. Embracing Faith

Mark's journey of faith deepened as he continued to explore and embrace his spirituality. He attended Bible study groups, participated in church activities, and found joy in serving others. His faith became the foundation of his life, guiding his decisions and actions.

Mark also developed a close friendship with Pastor John, who continued to mentor and support him. They often discussed scripture, theology, and the challenges of living a faith-centered life. Pastor John's wisdom and compassion were a constant source of encouragement and inspiration.

One evening, as they sat in the church office, Mark shared his reflections on his journey. "Pastor John, I never imagined that my life would take this path. I was lost and disillusioned, but now I feel a sense of purpose and peace that I never thought possible."

Pastor John smiled warmly. "Mark, your journey is a testament to the power of faith and the grace of God. You have listened to the Shepherd's voice and followed His guidance. Your story is an inspiration to others who may be struggling."

11. Sharing His Story

Inspired by his own transformation, Mark felt a calling to share his story with others. He believed that his experiences could offer hope and encouragement to those facing similar challenges. With Pastor John's support, Mark began speaking at church events and community gatherings.

He shared his journey of ambition, disillusionment, and redemption, emphasizing the importance of faith and the power of the Shepherd's voice. Mark's authenticity and vulnerability resonated with many, and he found fulfillment in helping others find their own paths of healing and growth.

Mark also started a blog, writing about his experiences and reflections on faith. His posts reached a wide audience, offering insights and encouragement to readers from all walks of life. The blog became a platform for Mark to connect with others, share his faith, and continue his journey of growth.

12. A Life of Purpose

As Mark's faith journey continued, he found a renewed sense of purpose in his personal and professional life. He approached his work with integrity and compassion, seeking to make a positive impact on his clients and colleagues. His balanced approach to life and work earned him respect and admiration from those around him.

Mark also dedicated time to volunteer work, supporting community outreach programs and helping those in need. He found joy and fulfillment in serving others, knowing that his actions reflected his faith and values.

One of the most meaningful projects Mark undertook was mentoring young professionals who were navigating the challenges of their careers and personal lives. He shared his experiences and offered guidance, helping them find balance, purpose, and faith.

13. The Power of Community

Throughout his journey, Mark discovered the importance of community. His relationships with family, friends, and church members provided a strong support system that helped him navigate the ups and downs of life.

The church community, in particular, became a source of strength and encouragement. Mark formed deep connections with fellow believers, sharing in their joys and challenges. Together, they supported each other, prayed for one another, and grew in their faith.

Pastor John's leadership and mentorship were instrumental in fostering a sense of unity and compassion within the church. His teachings emphasized the importance of love, grace, and service, values that resonated deeply with Mark and the entire congregation.

14. A Testimony of Faith

As Mark reflected on his journey, he felt a deep sense of gratitude for the people and experiences that had shaped his life. He knew that his story was a testament to the power of faith, the grace of God, and the resilience of the human spirit.

Mark's transformation from a lost and disillusioned man to a faith-centered and purposeful individual was a journey of redemption and growth. He had listened to the Shepherd's voice, trusted in God's plan, and followed His guidance, even when the path was difficult.

One Sunday, Mark was invited to share his testimony during a church service. Standing before the congregation, he felt a sense of humility and gratitude. He spoke about his journey, the challenges he had faced, and the transformative power of faith.

"God's grace is boundless," Mark said, his voice filled with conviction. "No matter how lost we may feel, He seeks us out and guides us back to His love. I am grateful for the Shepherd's voice that led me to a life of purpose and peace."

15. Continuing the Journey

Mark's journey of faith was ongoing, a continuous path of growth and discovery. He knew that life would bring new challenges and opportunities, but he faced the future with confidence, trusting in God's plan and the guidance of the Shepherd's voice.

He continued to serve his community, mentor others, and share his story, knowing that his experiences could offer hope and encouragement to those in need. Mark's life was a testament to the power of faith, the strength of community, and the resilience of the human spirit.

As he knelt in prayer each evening, Mark thanked God for His grace and guidance. He reflected on the journey he had undertaken, the people who had supported him, and the lessons he had learned. He knew that he was never alone, that the Shepherd's voice would always guide him, and that his faith would continue to be a source of strength and purpose.

Conclusion

"The Shepherd's Voice" in "Streams of Hope: An Anthology of Faith" tells the story of Mark Stevens, a lost and disillusioned man who finds hope and direction through a chance encounter with a compassionate pastor. Guided by the Shepherd's voice, Mark embarks on a journey of faith, redemption, and growth.

Mark's transformation from a life of ambition and emptiness to one of purpose and peace illustrates the power of faith and the grace of God. His story is grounded in the biblical verse John 10:27: "My sheep listen to my voice; I know them, and they follow me."

Through his journey, Mark discovers the importance of community, the strength of relationships, and the resilience of the human spirit. His testimony serves as a beacon of hope and encouragement, reminding us all that, no matter how lost we may feel, we are never alone. The Shepherd's voice is always there to guide us, offering a path to healing, growth, and fulfillment.

Chapter 5: Grace Under Fire

Bible Verse: Psalm 91:2 - "I will say of the Lord, 'He is my refuge and my fortress, my God, in whom I trust.'"

1. The Call to Duty

Sergeant David Turner had always felt a deep sense of duty and patriotism. Growing up in a military family, he was surrounded by stories of bravery and sacrifice. His father had served in Vietnam, and his grandfather in World War II. Inspired by their legacy, David enlisted in the Army right out of high school, determined to serve his country.

David's journey through basic training and subsequent deployments shaped him into a capable and resilient soldier. He quickly rose through the ranks, earning the respect of his peers and superiors. But amid the camaraderie and discipline of military life, David struggled with the spiritual challenges that came with the horrors of war.

2. The Deployment

David's latest deployment was to a conflict zone in the Middle East, a region plagued by violence and instability. The mission was fraught with danger, requiring constant vigilance and readiness. The harsh environment, the ever-present threat of attack, and the relentless pace of operations took a toll on both body and mind.

Before leaving for deployment, David's mother had given him a small pocket Bible, urging him to find strength in its pages. Though he appreciated the gesture, David had drifted from his faith over the years, relying more on his own strength and the bonds of brotherhood among his fellow soldiers.

3. The First Battle

The reality of war struck hard during David's first major engagement. His unit was ambushed while on patrol, and the ensuing firefight was chaotic and brutal.

Amid the deafening noise of gunfire and explosions, David saw comrades fall, their lives cut short by the violence of conflict.

In the heat of battle, David's training took over, and he fought with determination and skill. But as the dust settled and the adrenaline subsided, he was left with the haunting images of loss and the weight of survivor's guilt. That night, as he lay in his bunk, he felt an overwhelming sense of emptiness and despair.

David reached for the pocket Bible his mother had given him. Opening it at random, his eyes fell on Psalm 91:2: "I will say of the Lord, 'He is my refuge and my fortress, my God, in whom I trust.'" The words resonated deeply with him, offering a glimmer of hope and comfort amidst the chaos.

4. Finding Faith

In the days that followed, David began to turn to his Bible more frequently. The scriptures provided solace and strength, reminding him of the presence of a higher power in the midst of turmoil. He started to pray, seeking God's guidance and protection for himself and his fellow soldiers.

David's faith journey was not without its challenges. Doubts and fears often crept in, and the harsh realities of war tested his beliefs. But he found that prayer and scripture offered a source of stability and resilience, helping him navigate the emotional and psychological trials of combat.

His fellow soldiers noticed the change in David. He became a source of strength and encouragement, offering words of hope and comfort to those struggling with the same fears and anxieties. His faith became a beacon in the darkness, guiding not only himself but also those around him.

5. Brotherhood in Arms

The bonds of brotherhood in David's unit were strong. The shared experiences of training, combat, and loss forged deep connections among the soldiers. They relied on each other for support, knowing that their lives depended on their collective strength and trust.

David's faith added another layer to this bond. He began leading small prayer groups, where soldiers could come together to share their burdens and seek spiritual support. These gatherings became a source of comfort and unity, helping the soldiers find peace amidst the chaos of war.

One of David's closest friends, Corporal Mike Harris, was particularly impacted by these gatherings. Mike had struggled with his faith for years, questioning the existence of God in the face of suffering and loss. Through his friendship with David and the support of the prayer group, Mike began to rediscover his own faith, finding hope and strength in the shared journey.

6. The Chaplain

During one particularly difficult period, David's unit was stationed at a remote outpost, isolated from the main base and facing constant threats. The physical and emotional toll of the deployment was evident, and morale was low.

It was during this time that a chaplain, Lieutenant Colonel Samuel Rodriguez, visited the outpost. Chaplain Rodriguez was a seasoned veteran, having served in multiple deployments. His presence brought a sense of calm and reassurance to the weary soldiers.

David felt an immediate connection with Chaplain Rodriguez. They spent hours talking about faith, life, and the challenges of serving in the military. The chaplain's wisdom and compassion were a source of inspiration for David, reinforcing his commitment to his faith.

Chaplain Rodriguez also led worship services and offered counseling to the soldiers, providing a much-needed spiritual lifeline. His presence reminded the soldiers that they were not alone, that there was a higher power watching over them, offering strength and protection.

7. The Letter Home

One evening, David sat down to write a letter to his mother. He wanted to share with her the impact that the pocket Bible and her encouragement had on his journey. As he wrote, he reflected on the many ways his faith had sustained him through the trials of war.

"Dear Mom," he began, "I want to thank you for the Bible you gave me. It has been a source of comfort and strength in ways I never imagined. The words of Psalm 91:2 have been my refuge and fortress, reminding me to trust in God even in the darkest moments."

David shared stories of his experiences, the challenges he faced, and the ways his faith had grown. He expressed gratitude for the prayers and support of his family, knowing that their love and faith were with him every step of the way.

As he finished the letter, David felt a sense of peace. He knew that his journey was far from over, but he was confident in the strength of his faith and the presence of God in his life.

8. The Battle of Najaf

The Battle of Najaf was one of the most intense and harrowing experiences of David's deployment. The city, a strategic stronghold, was the site of fierce fighting between coalition forces and insurgents. David's unit was tasked with securing key positions and supporting the local population.

The fighting was brutal, with both sides sustaining heavy casualties. The constant threat of IEDs, snipers, and ambushes created a sense of perpetual danger. David's training and faith were put to the ultimate test as he navigated the chaos of urban combat.

During one particularly intense firefight, David's squad was pinned down by enemy fire. The situation seemed dire, and the possibility of survival appeared slim. In that moment of desperation, David felt a surge of determination and faith. He remembered the words of Psalm 91:2 and prayed for God's protection.

Miraculously, reinforcements arrived just in time, providing the cover needed for David's squad to escape. The experience reinforced his belief in the power of prayer and the presence of a higher power watching over them.

9. The Hospital

Despite their best efforts, the realities of war meant that injuries and loss were inevitable. David was wounded during a patrol, sustaining shrapnel injuries from an IED explosion. The pain was excruciating, and he was airlifted to a military hospital for treatment.

The hospital was filled with wounded soldiers, each with their own stories of bravery and sacrifice. David's recovery was slow and painful, both physically and emotionally. He struggled with feelings of guilt for leaving his comrades behind and anxiety about his future.

Chaplain Rodriguez visited David in the hospital, offering words of comfort and prayer. The chaplain's presence was a lifeline, helping David navigate the emotional challenges of recovery. They talked about faith, resilience, and the importance of finding purpose even in the face of adversity.

David also found support from his fellow patients. They shared their experiences, fears, and hopes, forming a bond of solidarity and mutual encouragement. Through their collective strength and faith, they found a sense of hope and healing.

10. A Visit from Home

During his recovery, David received a visit from his mother and sister. Their presence brought immense comfort and joy, reminding him of the love and support that awaited him at home. They talked for hours, sharing stories and expressing gratitude for the moments they had together.

David's mother brought with her a small cross, a symbol of their faith and a reminder of God's love. She placed it on his bedside table, where it became a source of strength and inspiration for David during his recovery.

His sister, Emma, shared stories of their hometown and the support of their community. She told him about the prayers and well-wishes from friends and neighbors, reminding David that he was not alone in his journey.

The visit from his family renewed David's determination to recover and return to his unit. He knew that his journey was far from over, but he was confident in the strength of his faith and the support of his loved ones.

11. Returning to the Front

After months of recovery and rehabilitation, David was cleared to return to his unit. The transition was challenging, as he had to rebuild his physical strength and adjust to the demands of military life. But his faith and determination carried him through.

His return was met with a mixture of relief and celebration from his comrades. They had missed his leadership and camaraderie, and his presence brought a renewed sense of unity and purpose to the unit.

David continued to rely on his faith, leading prayer groups and offering support to his fellow soldiers. He knew that the challenges of war were far from over, but he was committed to serving with honor and integrity, trusting in God's guidance and protection.

12. The Final Battle

The final months of David's deployment were marked by a series of intense battles as coalition forces sought to stabilize the region. The stakes were high, and the risks were ever-present. David's leadership and faith were put to the ultimate test.

One of the most significant battles took place in a remote village that had been overrun by insurgents. David's unit was tasked with liberating the village and providing humanitarian aid to its residents. The mission was complex and dangerous, requiring careful coordination and unwavering resolve.

As the battle unfolded, David found himself leading his squad through a series of fierce engagements. The fighting was intense, and the losses were heavy. But through it all, David remained steadfast in his faith, praying for strength and guidance.

In the heat of battle, David's squad encountered a group of civilians trapped in a building under heavy fire. Without hesitation, David led a daring rescue mission, providing cover for his men as they evacuated the civilians to safety. His bravery and leadership were instrumental in saving lives and securing the village.

13. The Homecoming

After a grueling deployment, David's unit was finally rotated out of the conflict zone and returned home. The homecoming was an emotional and joyous occasion, filled with reunions and celebrations. Families and friends gathered to welcome their loved ones back, expressing gratitude for their service and sacrifice.

David's homecoming was particularly poignant. He was greeted by his mother, sister, and a large contingent of friends and neighbors. The support and love of his community were overwhelming, reminding David of the strength and resilience of the bonds that had sustained him through the trials of war.

The transition to civilian life was challenging, as David adjusted to the pace and demands of a world far removed from the conflict zone. But his faith and the support of his loved ones provided a strong foundation, helping him navigate the complexities of reintegration.

14. Finding Purpose

As David settled into civilian life, he sought ways to channel his experiences and skills into meaningful work. He became involved in veteran support organizations, offering his time and expertise to help fellow veterans navigate the challenges of post-deployment life.

David also pursued higher education, earning a degree in counseling with a focus on trauma and resilience. His experiences in the military and his journey of faith gave him a unique perspective and deep empathy for those struggling with the aftermath of war.

Through his work as a counselor, David found a renewed sense of purpose. He helped veterans and their families find healing and hope, drawing on his own journey of faith and resilience. His commitment to service and compassion became a guiding force in his life.

15. A Testament of Faith

David's journey of faith and resilience became a testament to the power of God's grace and the strength of the human spirit. His experiences in the military, the challenges he faced, and the faith that sustained him were a source of inspiration for many.

He often shared his story with churches, community groups, and veteran organizations, emphasizing the importance of faith, resilience, and community support. David's authenticity and vulnerability resonated deeply with his audience, offering hope and encouragement to those facing their own battles.

One Sunday, David was invited to speak at his home church. Standing before the congregation, he reflected on his journey and the lessons he had learned. "Through the trials of war, I found strength in my faith and the presence of God. Psalm 91:2 reminds us that the Lord is our refuge and fortress, our source of trust and protection. No matter the challenges we face, we are never alone."

David's testimony was a powerful reminder of the enduring strength of faith and the resilience of the human spirit. His journey of grace under fire illustrated the timeless truth of Psalm 91:2 and offered a message of hope and healing to all who heard it.

Conclusion

"Grace Under Fire" in "Streams of Hope: An Anthology of Faith" tells the story of Sergeant David Turner, a soldier whose journey of faith sustains him through the trials of war. Guided by the words of Psalm 91:2, David finds hope and solace amidst the chaos, relying on God's protection and grace.

David's transformation from a soldier struggling with the horrors of war to a faith-centered and resilient individual illustrates the power of faith and the strength of the human spirit. His story is a testament to the presence of a higher power, offering guidance and protection in the darkest of times.

Through his journey, David discovers the importance of community, the bonds of brotherhood, and the resilience of faith. His testimony serves as a beacon of hope and encouragement, reminding us all that, no matter the challenges we face, we can find strength and protection in God's grace.

Chapter 6: The Light in the Darkness

Bible Verse: Psalm 34:18 - "The Lord is close to the brokenhearted and saves those who are crushed in spirit."

1. The Descent

Samantha Parker was once a vibrant and ambitious woman, filled with dreams and aspirations. A successful graphic designer in a bustling city, she had a promising career, a close circle of friends, and a loving family. From the outside, her life seemed perfect, but inside, Samantha was battling a darkness that threatened to consume her.

Depression had crept into Samantha's life gradually. What started as occasional feelings of sadness and fatigue slowly morphed into a relentless sense of hopelessness and despair. The pressures of her job, the strain of maintaining appearances, and unresolved personal traumas compounded her emotional turmoil. She felt like she was drowning, unable to breathe or find solid ground.

Samantha's friends and family noticed the change in her demeanor. She became withdrawn, missing social gatherings and avoiding conversations. At work, her performance suffered, and she found it increasingly difficult to concentrate or find joy in her creative projects. The once vibrant spark in her eyes was replaced by a dull, lifeless gaze.

Despite their concerns, Samantha's loved ones struggled to reach her. She put up walls, convinced that no one could understand her pain. She felt isolated, trapped in a cycle of negative thoughts and overwhelming emotions. Depression whispered lies into her ear, convincing her that she was alone, unloved, and beyond help.

2. The Breaking Point

One particularly bleak evening, Samantha hit rock bottom. The weight of her depression became unbearable, and she contemplated ending her life. The thought of escaping the pain was tempting, but a small, flickering spark of hope kept her from taking that final step. In her darkest moment, she cried out to God, desperate for relief and guidance.

"God, if you're there, please help me," she whispered through her tears. "I can't do this anymore. I need you."

The act of reaching out, even in her despair, marked a turning point for Samantha. Though she didn't feel an immediate change, the simple act of crying out to God planted a seed of hope in her heart. She realized that she couldn't face this battle alone and needed to seek help.

3. Seeking Help

The next day, Samantha mustered the courage to reach out to her older sister, Rachel. Rachel had always been a pillar of strength and faith in the family, and Samantha trusted her implicitly. Through tears, she shared her struggles and fears, opening up about the depth of her depression.

Rachel listened with compassion and empathy, her heart aching for her sister. She offered words of comfort and assurance, reminding Samantha that she was not alone and that help was available. Rachel encouraged Samantha to seek professional help and offered to support her through the process.

With Rachel's support, Samantha made an appointment with a therapist who specialized in depression and anxiety. The first few sessions were challenging, as she confronted painful memories and emotions. But gradually, she began to understand the underlying causes of her depression and learned strategies to manage her symptoms.

4. Rediscovering Faith

Rachel also invited Samantha to attend church with her. Though Samantha had grown up in a Christian family, her faith had waned over the years. The idea of returning to church was both comforting and intimidating. She feared judgment and doubted whether she could find solace in her faith again.

But Rachel's gentle encouragement and unwavering support convinced Samantha to give it a try. On a Sunday morning, they attended a service together. The atmosphere was warm and welcoming, and Samantha felt a sense of peace as she listened to the hymns and the pastor's sermon.

The pastor spoke about God's love and grace, emphasizing that He was close to the brokenhearted and saved those who were crushed in spirit. The words resonated deeply with Samantha, echoing the verse from Psalm 34:18 that Rachel had often quoted to her. She felt a glimmer of hope, a sense that maybe, just maybe, God had not abandoned her.

5. The Healing Journey

Samantha's journey of healing was neither quick nor easy. It was a process filled with ups and downs, moments of clarity and times of doubt. But she found strength in her faith and the support of her loved ones. She began to pray regularly, seeking God's guidance and comfort.

Prayer became a source of solace for Samantha. She poured out her heart to God, sharing her fears, frustrations, and hopes. In her quiet moments of prayer, she felt a sense of peace and reassurance, as if God was gently holding her hand and guiding her through the darkness.

Samantha also immersed herself in the scriptures, finding wisdom and encouragement in the Bible's pages. Verses about God's love, grace, and presence brought comfort and hope. She particularly resonated with Psalm 34:18, which reminded her that God was close to the brokenhearted and saved those who were crushed in spirit.

Her therapist, Dr. Mitchell, played a crucial role in her healing journey. With patience and expertise, Dr. Mitchell helped Samantha explore her emotions, identify negative thought patterns, and develop healthier coping mechanisms. Therapy sessions provided a safe space for Samantha to process her experiences and work towards healing.

6. Building a Support System

Samantha's support system extended beyond her family and therapist. She joined a support group for individuals struggling with depression and anxiety, where she met others who understood her pain and offered empathy and encouragement. The group became a source of strength, reminding her that she was not alone in her struggles.

Rachel continued to be a constant presence in Samantha's life. They attended church together, participated in Bible study groups, and spent quality time nurturing their sisterly bond. Rachel's unwavering faith and love were a lifeline for Samantha, providing stability and reassurance.

Samantha also reconnected with old friends and gradually rebuilt her social life. She learned to set boundaries and prioritize her well-being, surrounding herself with positive influences and nurturing relationships. The love and support of her friends became a source of joy and encouragement.

7. Embracing New Passions

As Samantha's mental health improved, she began to explore new passions and interests. She discovered a love for painting, finding it a therapeutic and expressive outlet. Art became a way for her to process her emotions and connect with her inner self.

She also started volunteering at a local community center, helping with programs for children and teens. The sense of purpose and fulfillment she found in serving others was transformative. It reminded her of the value of compassion and the impact of small acts of kindness.

Through these new passions, Samantha experienced moments of joy and fulfillment that she had long thought lost. She realized that healing was not just about overcoming depression but also about rediscovering the beauty and meaning in life.

8. Faith in Action

Samantha's renewed faith became a guiding force in her life. She felt a deep sense of gratitude for God's presence and grace, which had sustained her through her darkest moments. Her faith was no longer a distant memory but a living, breathing part of her daily existence.

She became more involved in her church, participating in outreach programs and supporting those in need. Samantha's experiences gave her a unique perspective and empathy, allowing her to connect with others who were struggling. Her journey of healing became a testimony of God's love and grace.

One of the most impactful experiences was her involvement in a church ministry that supported individuals battling mental health issues. Samantha shared her story, offering hope and encouragement to others. Her authenticity and vulnerability resonated deeply, and she became a source of inspiration for many.

9. Facing Challenges

Despite the progress she had made, Samantha's journey was not without its challenges. There were moments of doubt, setbacks, and days when the darkness seemed overwhelming. But she had learned to lean on her faith and support system, finding strength in the midst of adversity.

During particularly difficult times, Samantha found solace in the Psalms. The raw emotions and honest expressions of pain and hope in the scriptures mirrored her own struggles and reminded her that she was not alone. Psalm 34:18 remained a source of comfort, reinforcing the truth that God was close to her, even in her brokenness.

Samantha also continued her therapy sessions, recognizing the importance of ongoing support and self-care. Dr. Mitchell helped her navigate the complexities of her emotions, offering guidance and strategies to maintain her mental health.

10. A Transformative Encounter

One pivotal moment in Samantha's journey occurred during a church retreat. The retreat was focused on spiritual renewal and healing, providing a space for participants to connect with God and each other. Samantha was both excited and apprehensive about the experience, unsure of what to expect.

The retreat was held in a serene and picturesque location, surrounded by nature. The peaceful environment provided a stark contrast to the noise and busyness of city life. Samantha felt a sense of calm as she arrived, hopeful that the retreat would bring further healing and clarity.

Throughout the weekend, participants engaged in worship, prayer, and reflective activities. Samantha found herself deeply moved by the sense of community and the presence of God. She felt a renewed sense of connection to her faith and a deeper understanding of God's love.

One evening, during a time of guided prayer and meditation, Samantha had a transformative encounter. As she sat quietly, her eyes closed, she felt an overwhelming sense of peace wash over her. It was as if God was wrapping her in a warm embrace, assuring her of His love and presence.

In that moment, Samantha felt a profound release of the pain and burden she had carried for so long. Tears streamed down her face as she experienced a deep sense of healing and renewal. She realized that God had been with her every step of the way, guiding her through the darkness and leading her to the light.

11. Embracing a New Identity

The retreat marked a turning point in Samantha's journey. She returned home with a renewed sense of purpose and identity. She no longer defined

herself by her struggles with depression but by her resilience, faith, and the love of God that had sustained her.

Samantha embraced her new identity as a child of God, deeply loved and valued. She found joy in her daily life, appreciating the small moments of beauty and connection. Her faith became a source of strength and inspiration, guiding her decisions and actions.

She also continued to pursue her passions, finding fulfillment in her creative endeavors and volunteer work. Her art blossomed, reflecting the depth of her emotions and the journey she had undertaken. Her paintings became a testament to the healing power of creativity and faith.

12. A Source of Inspiration

Samantha's journey of healing and faith inspired many around her. She became a sought-after speaker, sharing her story at churches, conferences, and community events. Her authenticity and vulnerability resonated with audiences, offering hope and encouragement to those facing their own battles.

She also wrote a book about her experiences, detailing her journey from darkness to light. The book, titled "The Light in the Darkness," became a source of inspiration for readers, reminding them of the power of faith and the presence of God in their lives.

Samantha's story reached a wide audience, touching the hearts of many who felt alone and overwhelmed by their struggles. Her message was clear: no matter how deep the darkness, God's light could penetrate and bring healing and hope.

13. A Life Transformed

As Samantha reflected on her journey, she felt a deep sense of gratitude for the transformation she had experienced. She had moved from a place of despair to one of hope, from isolation to connection, and from darkness to light. Her faith had been the guiding force, providing strength and comfort in the midst of her struggles.

Samantha's life was a testament to the truth of Psalm 34:18: "The Lord is close to the brokenhearted and saves those who are crushed in spirit." Her journey illustrated the power of God's love and grace to bring healing and renewal.

She continued to live her life with purpose and passion, guided by her faith and the desire to help others. Samantha knew that her journey was ongoing, but she faced the future with confidence, trusting in God's presence and guidance.

14. Giving Back

One of the most fulfilling aspects of Samantha's journey was her commitment to giving back to her community. She started a non-profit organization dedicated to supporting individuals struggling with mental health issues. The organization provided counseling, support groups, and resources, helping people find hope and healing.

Samantha's leadership and vision were instrumental in the success of the organization. She worked tirelessly to raise awareness about mental health and reduce the stigma surrounding it. Her efforts made a significant impact, providing much-needed support to countless individuals and families.

Through her work, Samantha found a deep sense of fulfillment and purpose. She knew that her experiences had equipped her to make a difference in the lives of others, and she was grateful for the opportunity to serve and support her community.

15. A Testament of Faith

Samantha's journey of healing and faith became a testament to the power of God's love and grace. Her story was a beacon of hope, reminding others that they were not alone in their struggles and that healing was possible.

She continued to share her story, offering encouragement and support to those facing their own battles. Her faith remained the foundation of her life, guiding her actions and providing strength and comfort.

One Sunday, Samantha was invited to share her testimony during a church service. Standing before the congregation, she reflected on her journey and the lessons she had learned.

"God's love and grace have been my guiding light," she said, her voice filled with conviction. "Through the darkest moments, I found strength in His presence and hope in His promises. Psalm 34:18 reminds us that the Lord is close to the brokenhearted and saves those who are crushed in spirit. No matter how deep the darkness, His light can bring healing and renewal."

Samantha's testimony was a powerful reminder of the enduring strength of faith and the resilience of the human spirit. Her journey from darkness to light illustrated the transformative power of God's love and grace, offering a message of hope and healing to all who heard it.

Conclusion

"The Light in the Darkness" in "Streams of Hope: An Anthology of Faith" tells the story of Samantha Parker, a woman battling depression who finds hope and healing through her renewed relationship with God. Guided by the words of Psalm 34:18, Samantha's journey illustrates the power of faith to bring light to the darkest moments and provide strength and comfort to the brokenhearted.

Samantha's transformation from a place of despair to one of hope and purpose is a testament to the presence of God and the power of His love. Her story serves as a beacon of hope and inspiration, reminding us all that, no matter how deep the darkness, God's light can bring healing and renewal.

Through her journey, Samantha discovers the importance of faith, community, and compassion. Her testimony offers encouragement and support to those facing their own battles, illustrating the truth that the Lord is close to the brokenhearted and saves those who are crushed in spirit.

Chapter 7: Blessed Beginnings

Bible Verse: Jeremiah 29:11 - "'For I know the plans I have for you,' declares the Lord, 'plans to prosper you and not to harm you, plans to give you hope and a future.'"

1. The Dream of Parenthood

Rachel and Michael Johnson had always dreamed of becoming parents. From the moment they met, they shared a deep desire to build a family together. Their love story was one of mutual respect, unwavering support, and a shared faith that guided them through life's challenges.

After marrying, Rachel and Michael looked forward to the day they would welcome a child into their lives. They imagined the joy of holding their baby for the first time, watching their first steps, and sharing in the countless milestones that mark the journey of parenthood. But as months turned into years, their dream remained unfulfilled.

2. The Struggle with Infertility

The path to parenthood proved more difficult than Rachel and Michael had ever imagined. Despite their best efforts, Rachel struggled to conceive. Each month brought a fresh wave of hope followed by crushing disappointment. The emotional toll was immense, and the couple found themselves grappling with feelings of sadness, frustration, and inadequacy.

The Johnsons sought medical advice, undergoing numerous tests and treatments. They endured the physical and emotional strain of fertility treatments, only to be met with repeated failures. The medical explanations were elusive, leaving them with more questions than answers. It was a journey fraught with pain and uncertainty.

Rachel and Michael leaned on each other for support, their bond growing stronger even as they faced the heartache of infertility. They prayed together, seeking comfort and guidance from God. Their faith, though tested, remained a source of strength and hope.

3. The Turning Point

One particularly difficult evening, after yet another failed treatment, Rachel found herself in tears, overwhelmed by a sense of hopelessness. Michael held her close, his heart breaking for his wife. He wanted to fix everything, to take away her pain, but felt powerless in the face of their struggle.

"Rachel," Michael said softly, "we have to trust that God has a plan for us. I don't know what it is, but I believe He has something beautiful in store for us. Jeremiah 29:11 says, 'For I know the plans I have for you,' declares the Lord, 'plans to prosper you and not to harm you, plans to give you hope and a future.' Let's hold on to that promise."

Rachel nodded through her tears, finding comfort in Michael's words. They knelt together and prayed, asking God for clarity and peace. It was a moment of surrender, a recognition that they could not control their path but could trust in God's plan.

4. The Seed of Adoption

As Rachel and Michael continued to pray and seek guidance, the idea of adoption began to take root in their hearts. It was a thought that had crossed their minds before, but now it seemed to grow stronger, fueled by a sense of divine purpose.

They began to research adoption, learning about the process, the challenges, and the incredible stories of families who had found joy and fulfillment through adopting children. The more they learned, the more they felt drawn to the idea. It was as if God was gently guiding them towards a new path, one they had not previously considered.

One Sunday, their pastor gave a sermon on the theme of God's plans and the ways He works through our lives. He spoke of the unexpected paths that can lead to the greatest blessings, and how faith and trust in God can open doors to new possibilities. Rachel and Michael felt a deep resonance with his words, sensing that God was speaking directly to them.

5. Embracing the Journey

With renewed hope and a sense of purpose, Rachel and Michael decided to pursue adoption. They began the process with a mixture of excitement and apprehension, knowing that it would be a journey filled with its own challenges and uncertainties. But they felt a deep sense of peace, believing that they were following God's plan for their lives.

The adoption process was rigorous and demanding. They underwent background checks, home studies, and numerous interviews. They prepared their home and their hearts for the arrival of a child, embracing each step with faith and determination.

Throughout the process, Rachel and Michael leaned on their faith and their support system. Their family, friends, and church community rallied around them, offering prayers, encouragement, and practical help. It was a testament to the power of community and the strength that comes from shared faith.

6. The Waiting Period

The waiting period was both challenging and transformative for Rachel and Michael. They learned to be patient, to trust in God's timing, and to find joy in the present moment. It was a time of growth and reflection, a period of preparation for the blessings to come.

During this time, Rachel and Michael continued to deepen their faith. They attended church regularly, participated in Bible study groups, and found comfort in the scriptures. Jeremiah 29:11 became a cornerstone of their faith journey, a constant reminder of God's promise and plan for their lives.

They also took the opportunity to strengthen their relationship, spending quality time together and nurturing their bond. They knew that their love and unity would be the foundation for the family they hoped to build.

7. The Call

One crisp autumn morning, Rachel and Michael received the call that would change their lives forever. Their adoption agency informed them that they had been matched with a newborn baby girl. The birth mother had chosen them to be the parents of her child, and the baby was due to be born in a few weeks.

Rachel and Michael were overwhelmed with emotion. They felt a mixture of joy, gratitude, and nervous anticipation. They had prayed for this moment, and now it was finally here. They thanked God for His faithfulness and for guiding them to this new beginning.

The next few weeks were a whirlwind of preparation and excitement. They readied the nursery, bought baby clothes and supplies, and made plans for the baby's arrival. They also continued to pray, asking God for wisdom, strength, and grace as they embarked on this new chapter.

8. Meeting Their Daughter

The day their daughter was born was a day Rachel and Michael would never forget. They were at the hospital, filled with nervous excitement and anticipation. When the nurse placed the tiny, swaddled baby in Rachel's arms, tears streamed down her face. Michael stood by her side, his heart full of love and gratitude.

They named their daughter Grace, a testament to the divine favor and love that had brought her into their lives. Holding Grace for the first time, Rachel and Michael felt a profound sense of fulfillment and joy. It was a moment of pure grace, a blessing that surpassed their greatest hopes.

They spent the first few days in awe of their precious daughter, marveling at her tiny fingers and toes, her soft cries, and the way she fit perfectly into their arms. It was a time of bonding, of getting to know their new family member, and of giving thanks for the incredible gift they had been given.

9. Navigating Parenthood

The journey of parenthood was filled with both joys and challenges. Rachel and Michael faced sleepless nights, diaper changes, and the myriad demands of caring for a newborn. But every moment, even the difficult ones, was a reminder of the blessing that Grace was in their lives.

Their faith continued to be a guiding force, providing strength and wisdom as they navigated the ups and downs of parenthood. They prayed for Grace, asking God to watch over her, guide her, and fill her life with love and joy. They also prayed for themselves, seeking patience, wisdom, and grace in their roles as parents.

Rachel and Michael found support in their community, drawing on the love and wisdom of family and friends. They attended parenting classes, sought advice from experienced parents, and leaned on their church community for encouragement and prayer. It was a collective journey, filled with shared joys and challenges.

10. The Birth Mother's Story

As Grace grew, Rachel and Michael also sought to honor the woman who had given birth to their daughter. They wanted Grace to know her story, to understand the love and sacrifice that had brought her into their family. They reached out to the birth mother, Sarah, expressing their gratitude and offering to stay in touch if she wished.

Sarah was touched by their kindness and openness. She shared her own story, explaining the difficult decision she had made and the deep love she felt for her child. She was grateful that Grace had found a loving and faithful family, and she appreciated the opportunity to stay connected in a way that felt comfortable for everyone.

Rachel and Michael kept Sarah's story alive for Grace, incorporating it into their family narrative. They wanted Grace to grow up knowing that she was loved not only by them but also by her birth mother. It was a story of grace and love, a testament to the ways God works through our lives.

11. Celebrating Milestones

As the years passed, Rachel and Michael celebrated countless milestones with Grace. Her first steps, first words, and first day of school were moments of joy and pride. They cherished the small, everyday moments as well—the bedtime stories, the family meals, and the laughter that filled their home.

Their faith remained central to their family life. They attended church together, prayed as a family, and taught Grace about God's love and grace. Jeremiah 29:11 continued to be a guiding verse, reminding them of God's plans and promises.

Rachel and Michael also shared their story with others, offering encouragement and hope to couples facing infertility. They spoke about the ways God had guided them to adoption, the blessings they had received, and the joy of following God's plan. Their testimony was a source of inspiration for many, illustrating the power of faith and trust.

12. Grace's Journey

As Grace grew, she became a vibrant and curious child, filled with energy and enthusiasm. She loved hearing stories about her adoption, about the ways God had brought her into her family. Rachel and Michael nurtured her faith, encouraging her to explore and grow in her relationship with God.

Grace's journey was marked by her own moments of discovery and growth. She asked questions about her birth mother, her adoption, and her place in God's plan. Rachel and Michael answered her questions with honesty and love, helping her understand the beautiful and unique story of her life.

They also encouraged Grace to develop her own passions and interests. She loved music, art, and nature, and her parents supported her in pursuing these activities. They saw in her a reflection of God's creativity and joy, and they nurtured her gifts with love and encouragement.

13. Embracing God's Plan

Rachel and Michael's journey of faith and parenthood was a testament to the power of embracing God's plan. They had faced challenges and heartache, but through it all, they had discovered the joy and fulfillment that came from trusting in God's promises.

They continued to grow in their faith, seeking to live out the principles of love, grace, and compassion in their daily lives. They found joy in serving others, in supporting their community, and in nurturing their family. Their story was a testament to the ways God works through our lives, guiding us to unexpected blessings and new beginnings.

Rachel and Michael also felt a calling to support other families going through the adoption process. They became involved in adoption advocacy, offering their time, resources, and support to help others navigate the journey.

Their own experiences had equipped them to offer empathy, guidance, and encouragement.

14. A Testimony of Faith

One Sunday, Rachel and Michael were invited to share their testimony during a church service. Standing before the congregation, they reflected on their journey, the challenges they had faced, and the incredible blessings they had received.

"God's plan for us was different from what we had imagined," Rachel said, her voice filled with emotion. "But it was a plan filled with grace, love, and joy. Jeremiah 29:11 has been our guiding verse, reminding us that God knows the plans He has for us, plans to prosper us and not to harm us, plans to give us hope and a future."

Michael nodded in agreement. "Through our journey, we have learned to trust in God's timing and His wisdom. Adoption has brought us the greatest joy and fulfillment, and we are grateful for the ways God has worked in our lives. Grace is our precious blessing, a testament to God's love and faithfulness."

Their testimony resonated deeply with the congregation, offering hope and encouragement to those facing their own challenges. Rachel and Michael's story illustrated the power of faith, the beauty of God's plans, and the joy of embracing new beginnings.

15. Continuing the Journey

Rachel, Michael, and Grace continued their journey together, guided by their faith and the love that bound them as a family. They faced new challenges and celebrated new milestones, always trusting in God's presence and guidance.

Their home was filled with love, laughter, and the joy of shared experiences. They nurtured Grace's faith, encouraging her to explore her relationship with God and to discover her own path in life. They found fulfillment in their roles as parents, grateful for the blessings they had received.

Rachel and Michael also continued their advocacy work, supporting families and children in need. They saw their journey as a testament to the ways God works through our lives, bringing us to unexpected blessings and new beginnings.

As they knelt in prayer each evening, they thanked God for His faithfulness and love. They reflected on the journey they had undertaken, the challenges they had faced, and the incredible blessings they had received. They knew that their journey was ongoing, but they faced the future with confidence, trusting in God's presence and guidance.

Conclusion

"Blessed Beginnings" in "Streams of Hope: An Anthology of Faith" tells the story of Rachel and Michael Johnson, a couple facing infertility who discover the joy of adoption through their renewed faith. Guided by the words of Jeremiah 29:11, their journey illustrates the power of trusting in God's plans and embracing the unexpected blessings that come from faith.

Rachel and Michael's transformation from a place of heartache and struggle to one of joy and fulfillment is a testament to the presence of God and the power of His love. Their story serves as a beacon of hope and inspiration, reminding us all that, no matter the challenges we face, we can find strength and joy in God's plans.

Through their journey, Rachel and Michael discover the importance of faith, community, and compassion. Their testimony offers encouragement and support to those facing their own battles, illustrating the truth that God's plans are filled with hope, prosperity, and new beginnings.

Chapter 8: From Ashes to Beauty

Bible Verse: Isaiah 61:3 - "To bestow on them a crown of beauty instead of ashes, the oil of joy instead of mourning, and a garment of praise instead of a spirit of despair."

1. The Tragedy

The town of Green Valley was known for its close-knit community and picturesque landscapes. Nestled among rolling hills and dense forests, it was a place where neighbors knew each other by name, and the sense of belonging was palpable. Life in Green Valley was peaceful and predictable, until a devastating fire changed everything.

The fire started on a hot, dry summer day. Strong winds fanned the flames, which quickly spread through the forest and into the town. Despite the best efforts of firefighters and emergency responders, the fire ravaged homes, businesses, and landmarks, leaving behind a trail of destruction. Families were displaced, and the once vibrant community was shrouded in smoke and ash.

In the aftermath, Green Valley was unrecognizable. Charred remains of buildings and scorched earth replaced the familiar sights of home. The community was in shock, grappling with the magnitude of their loss. The fire had not only destroyed physical structures but also shattered the sense of security and normalcy that residents had taken for granted.

2. The Immediate Response

As the smoke cleared, the residents of Green Valley faced the daunting task of rebuilding their lives. The initial response was marked by a mixture of grief, confusion, and a desperate need for support. Shelters were set up for those who had lost their homes, and aid organizations arrived to provide food, clothing, and medical assistance.

Amid the chaos, a sense of solidarity began to emerge. Neighbors checked on each other, offering words of comfort and practical help. The local church, led by Pastor Samuel, became a hub of activity, organizing relief efforts and providing a space for the community to come together.

Pastor Samuel was a pillar of strength for Green Valley. His calm demeanor and unwavering faith offered reassurance to those who felt lost and overwhelmed. He reminded the community of Isaiah 61:3, encouraging them to hold on to hope and to trust that beauty would rise from the ashes of their despair.

3. The Healing Process Begins

The healing process was slow and fraught with challenges. Families mourned the loss of their homes and cherished belongings, while business owners faced the daunting task of rebuilding their livelihoods. The emotional toll was immense, and the path to recovery seemed insurmountable.

Pastor Samuel and the church played a crucial role in supporting the community. They organized prayer meetings, counseling sessions, and support groups, providing a safe space for people to express their grief and find solace in their shared faith. The church's message of hope and resilience resonated deeply, offering a beacon of light in the darkness.

One of the most impactful initiatives was the "Rebuild Green Valley" campaign. Spearheaded by the church and supported by local leaders, the campaign aimed to coordinate rebuilding efforts, raise funds, and mobilize volunteers. The community rallied together, driven by a collective determination to restore their town and rebuild their lives.

4. Stories of Resilience

Amid the devastation, stories of resilience and courage began to emerge. Families who had lost everything found strength in their faith and each other. Neighbors supported one another, sharing resources and offering practical help. These acts of kindness and solidarity became the foundation of Green Valley's recovery.

The Johnson family was one such example. Their home had been completely destroyed, and they had lost all their possessions. Despite the immense loss, they remained hopeful, drawing strength from their faith and the support of their community. They volunteered tirelessly in the relief efforts, helping others even as they navigated their own challenges.

Another story of resilience came from Maria Sanchez, a single mother who had lost her bakery to the fire. The bakery had been her dream and her sole source of income. Though devastated, Maria refused to give up. With the support of her church and neighbors, she began to rebuild, driven by a fierce determination to rise from the ashes.

5. Rebuilding Together

The process of rebuilding Green Valley was a monumental task that required coordination, resources, and a collective effort. Volunteers from neighboring towns and even other states arrived to lend a hand, bringing with them tools, supplies, and a spirit of solidarity.

Local businesses, despite their own losses, donated materials and services. Fundraisers were organized, and donations poured in from across the country. The "Rebuild Green Valley" campaign gained momentum, fueled by the unwavering determination of the community and the support of their allies.

Pastor Samuel and the church continued to be a guiding force. They coordinated volunteer efforts, provided logistical support, and offered spiritual guidance. The church's message of hope and resilience was a constant source of inspiration, reminding everyone that, with faith and unity, they could overcome even the greatest challenges.

6. The Role of Faith

Faith played a central role in Green Valley's recovery. The teachings of the Bible, particularly Isaiah 61:3, offered a framework for understanding and navigating the tragedy. The community found comfort in the promise that God would bestow beauty instead of ashes, joy instead of mourning, and praise instead of despair.

Prayer became a source of strength and solace. Residents gathered regularly to pray for guidance, healing, and hope. These gatherings fostered a sense of connection and solidarity, reinforcing the belief that they were not alone in their struggles.

The church also organized Bible study groups and workshops focused on themes of resilience, hope, and faith. These sessions provided a space for residents to explore their faith, share their experiences, and find strength in the scriptures. The words of Isaiah 61:3 became a mantra, a reminder of God's promise and presence.

7. New Beginnings

As the months passed, the landscape of Green Valley began to change. New homes and buildings rose from the ashes, a testament to the community's resilience and determination. The process was slow and challenging, but each step forward was a victory, a symbol of hope and renewal.

The Johnson family moved into their new home, grateful for the support and love that had carried them through. They held a housewarming celebration, inviting neighbors and friends to share in their joy. It was a moment of triumph, a reminder that even in the face of devastation, beauty could emerge.

Maria Sanchez reopened her bakery, a symbol of perseverance and hope. The new bakery, aptly named "Rising from the Ashes," became a gathering place for the community, a place where people could find comfort and connection. Maria's story inspired others, a testament to the power of faith and determination.

8. A Stronger Community

The fire had tested Green Valley in ways that no one could have imagined. But through the trials and challenges, the community emerged stronger and more united. The bonds forged in the aftermath of the fire were deep and enduring, a testament to the power of solidarity and faith.

Residents found new ways to support and uplift one another. Community events, fundraisers, and volunteer efforts became a regular part of life in Green Valley. The church continued to be a central hub, providing spiritual guidance, support, and a space for connection.

The "Rebuild Green Valley" campaign evolved into an ongoing initiative focused on community development and resilience. The lessons learned from the fire became the foundation for new projects and programs aimed at strengthening the community and preparing for future challenges.

9. Healing Through Service

Service to others became a cornerstone of Green Valley's recovery. Residents who had experienced loss and suffering found healing in helping others. Volunteering, supporting neighbors, and participating in community projects offered a sense of purpose and fulfillment.

The church's outreach programs expanded, offering support to neighboring communities facing their own challenges. The spirit of solidarity and compassion that had defined Green Valley's recovery became a guiding principle, inspiring others to join in the efforts to rebuild and uplift.

One of the most impactful initiatives was the "Ashes to Beauty" program, which provided resources, counseling, and support to families affected by the fire. The program emphasized the importance of faith, resilience, and community, offering a holistic approach to recovery and healing.

10. Reflecting on the Journey

As the community of Green Valley reflected on their journey, they recognized the profound impact of their shared faith and collective efforts. The fire had been a devastating tragedy, but it had also revealed the strength, resilience, and compassion that defined their community.

Pastor Samuel often spoke about the transformative power of faith and the promise of Isaiah 61:3. "God has turned our ashes into beauty," he would say, "and our mourning into joy. We have found strength in our faith and in each other, and we will continue to rise, no matter the challenges we face."

The stories of resilience, courage, and hope became a source of inspiration for the entire community. The journey from ashes to beauty was a testament to the power of faith, the strength of community, and the enduring promise of God's love.

11. A Testament of Faith

Green Valley's story of recovery and renewal became a testament to the power of faith and the promise of Isaiah 61:3. The community's journey from ashes to beauty illustrated the profound impact of faith, resilience, and solidarity.

Residents shared their stories with others, offering encouragement and hope to those facing their own challenges. The message was clear: no matter the devastation, no matter the loss, God's promise of beauty, joy, and praise would prevail.

The church compiled these stories into a book titled "From Ashes to Beauty," capturing the experiences, lessons, and faith that had defined Green Valley's recovery. The book became a source of inspiration for many, a testament to the enduring power of faith and community.

12. A Renewed Sense of Purpose

As Green Valley continued to rebuild, the community embraced a renewed sense of purpose. The fire had changed them, but it had also revealed their strength, resilience, and capacity for compassion. The lessons learned from their journey became the foundation for a stronger, more united community.

The "Rebuild Green Valley" campaign evolved into a permanent initiative focused on community development, resilience, and preparedness. Projects aimed at strengthening infrastructure, supporting local businesses, and fostering community engagement became central to the town's vision for the future.

Residents found new ways to connect, support, and uplift one another. The bonds forged in the aftermath of the fire were deep and enduring, a testament to the power of faith and solidarity. The church continued to play a central role, providing spiritual guidance, support, and a space for connection.

13. Celebrating Milestones

The journey from ashes to beauty was marked by countless milestones and moments of triumph. Each new home, each rebuilt business, and each community event was a symbol of hope and renewal. The residents of Green

Valley celebrated these milestones with joy and gratitude, recognizing the significance of each step forward.

One of the most significant celebrations was the grand reopening of the town square. The square had been a central gathering place before the fire, and its restoration was a symbol of Green Valley's resilience and renewal. The community gathered for a festive event, filled with music, food, and the shared joy of new beginnings.

Pastor Samuel gave a heartfelt speech, reflecting on the journey and the promise of Isaiah 61:3. "We have risen from the ashes," he said, "and we have found beauty, joy, and praise in our faith and in each other. Let us continue to build on this foundation, trusting in God's promise and working together to create a future filled with hope and strength."

14. The Legacy of Faith and Resilience

The legacy of Green Valley's recovery was defined by faith, resilience, and the enduring promise of God's love. The community's journey from devastation to renewal illustrated the transformative power of faith and the strength of solidarity.

Residents shared their experiences and lessons with others, offering guidance and support to communities facing their own challenges. The story of Green Valley became a beacon of hope, a testament to the ways in which faith and community could overcome even the greatest obstacles.

The church continued to play a central role, providing spiritual guidance, support, and a space for connection. The teachings of Isaiah 61:3 remained a cornerstone of their faith, a constant reminder of God's promise to turn ashes into beauty and mourning into joy.

15. Looking to the Future

As Green Valley looked to the future, the community embraced a vision of resilience, compassion, and hope. The journey from ashes to beauty had revealed their strength and capacity for renewal, and they were committed to building on this foundation.

The "Rebuild Green Valley" initiative continued to evolve, focusing on long-term development, community engagement, and preparedness. Projects aimed at strengthening infrastructure, supporting local businesses, and fostering a sense of unity and purpose became central to the town's vision.

Residents found new ways to connect, support, and uplift one another. The bonds forged in the aftermath of the fire were deep and enduring, a testament to the power of faith and solidarity. The church continued to be a guiding force, providing spiritual guidance and support.

As they knelt in prayer each evening, the residents of Green Valley thanked God for His faithfulness and love. They reflected on the journey they had undertaken, the challenges they had faced, and the incredible blessings they had received. They knew that their journey was ongoing, but they faced the future with confidence, trusting in God's presence and guidance.

Conclusion

"From Ashes to Beauty" in "Streams of Hope: An Anthology of Faith" tells the story of Green Valley, a community devastated by fire that comes together to rebuild, finding hope and strength in their shared faith. Guided by the words of Isaiah 61:3, their journey illustrates the power of faith to transform devastation into renewal, and despair into joy.

The transformation from a place of devastation to one of hope and renewal is a testament to the presence of God and the power of His love. Their story serves as a beacon of hope and inspiration, reminding us all that, no matter the challenges we face, we can find strength and joy in God's promises.

Through their journey, the residents of Green Valley discover the importance of faith, community, and compassion. Their testimony offers encouragement and support to those facing their own battles, illustrating the truth that God's promise of beauty, joy, and praise will prevail, even in the darkest of times.

Chapter 9: The Power of Forgiveness

Bible Verse: Ephesians 4:32 - "Be kind and compassionate to one another, forgiving each other, just as in Christ God forgave you."

1. The Burden of Grudges

James Thompson was a man carrying a heavy burden. He was known among his friends and family as someone who held grudges tightly, unable to let go of the wrongs he felt had been done to him. Over the years, these unresolved feelings of anger and resentment had weighed him down, affecting his relationships and overall well-being.

James grew up in a small town where everyone knew each other. In his early years, he was a happy, trusting boy, always ready to help others and eager to make friends. But life had thrown several painful experiences his way, gradually transforming his open heart into one guarded by thick walls of bitterness and distrust.

2. The Origins of Resentment

The roots of James's resentment could be traced back to several significant events in his life. The first major blow came during his teenage years when his best friend, Tom, betrayed his trust. Tom had spread a hurtful rumor about James that led to him being ostracized by his peers. The humiliation and hurt from this betrayal left a deep scar on James's heart.

Years later, James faced another betrayal, this time in his professional life. He had worked tirelessly to secure a promotion, only to have it given to a less qualified colleague who happened to be the boss's nephew. This incident reinforced his belief that trust and hard work were often unrewarded, further fueling his resentment.

The final straw came when his long-term relationship ended abruptly. James's girlfriend, Emily, left him for someone else, leaving him heartbroken and disillusioned. The cumulative weight of these experiences left James feeling isolated and bitter, unable to trust or forgive.

3. The Strain on Relationships

James's inability to forgive affected all aspects of his life, particularly his relationships. He became distant from his family, often lashing out at them in frustration. His friendships suffered as well, as he struggled to open up and trust others. His colleagues at work found him difficult to approach, and he often found himself isolated and alone.

The bitterness that had taken root in James's heart manifested in various ways. He was quick to anger, constantly on the defensive, and suspicious of others' intentions. His once cheerful demeanor had been replaced by a hardened exterior, and his world became increasingly small and lonely.

James's mother, Mary, was particularly concerned about him. She had watched her son's transformation with a heavy heart, knowing that the weight of his unresolved pain was consuming him. She often tried to reach out to him, encouraging him to find peace and healing through faith, but James dismissed her efforts, convinced that forgiveness was a sign of weakness.

4. A Chance Encounter

One Sunday morning, Mary convinced James to attend church with her. Reluctantly, he agreed, more to appease his mother than out of any genuine desire to reconnect with his faith. The sermon that day was about forgiveness, and the pastor's words struck a chord with James, though he was not ready to admit it.

After the service, Mary introduced James to Pastor David, a kind and compassionate man who had a gift for connecting with people. Pastor David sensed the heaviness in James's heart and invited him to join a small group discussion later that week. Despite his initial reluctance, James found himself agreeing to attend.

The small group discussion was centered around the theme of forgiveness and healing. As James listened to others share their stories of hurt and reconciliation, he felt a glimmer of hope. For the first time, he began to entertain the possibility that forgiveness might be a path to freedom rather than a sign of weakness.

5. The First Steps Toward Forgiveness

Encouraged by the small group discussion, James decided to meet with Pastor David one-on-one. During their conversation, he opened up about the betrayals and hurts that had shaped his life. Pastor David listened patiently, offering empathy and understanding.

"James," Pastor David said gently, "forgiveness is not about condoning the wrongs that have been done to you. It's about freeing yourself from the burden of resentment and allowing God's grace to heal your heart. Ephesians 4:32 reminds us to be kind and compassionate, forgiving each other just as Christ forgave us. Forgiveness is a gift you give yourself."

James was deeply moved by Pastor David's words. He realized that holding onto his anger and bitterness was only hurting himself. It was time to take the first steps toward forgiveness, even if it felt difficult and uncertain.

6. Confronting the Past

James knew that he needed to confront the people who had wronged him if he was to truly forgive and heal. The first person he reached out to was Tom, his childhood friend who had betrayed him. They met at a local coffee shop, and the conversation was awkward at first.

"Tom," James began, "I've carried a lot of anger towards you for what happened all those years ago. Your actions hurt me deeply, and I've struggled to let go of that pain. But I'm here because I want to forgive you and move forward."

Tom was taken aback by James's openness. He apologized sincerely, expressing regret for his actions and the pain they had caused. The conversation was emotional, but by the end, both men felt a sense of relief and closure. It was a significant step towards healing for James.

Next, James addressed the betrayal he experienced at work. He arranged a meeting with his former boss, Mr. Anderson, to discuss the promotion he had lost. Though it was challenging, James expressed his feelings honestly, seeking understanding and closure.

Mr. Anderson admitted that the decision had been influenced by nepotism and apologized for the unfairness James had experienced. This acknowledgment allowed James to release some of the resentment he had carried for so long. He realized that holding onto his anger had only hindered his own growth and happiness.

7. Rebuilding Trust

Forgiving Emily, his ex-girlfriend, was perhaps the most difficult step for James. The pain of their breakup had left deep emotional wounds, and he struggled to let go of the hurt. With Pastor David's guidance, James wrote a letter to Emily, expressing his feelings and his desire to forgive.

In the letter, James acknowledged the pain of their breakup but also recognized the need to release the bitterness he had been holding onto. He wished her well and expressed his hope that they could both find happiness and peace.

Writing the letter was a cathartic experience for James. It allowed him to confront his emotions and take a significant step towards healing. While he didn't receive a response from Emily, he felt a sense of closure and relief, knowing that he had taken the initiative to forgive and move forward.

8. Finding Peace Through Faith

As James continued his journey of forgiveness, he found himself drawing closer to his faith. He attended church regularly, participated in Bible study groups, and sought guidance from Pastor David. The teachings of the Bible, particularly Ephesians 4:32, became a source of inspiration and strength.

James also began to pray more frequently, seeking God's guidance and grace. Through prayer, he found comfort and reassurance, knowing that he was not alone in his journey. God's love and compassion became a guiding force, helping him navigate the complexities of forgiveness and healing.

One evening, as James knelt in prayer, he felt a profound sense of peace wash over him. It was as if a weight had been lifted from his shoulders, and he realized that forgiveness had brought him freedom. He thanked God for His grace and for the strength to forgive those who had wronged him.

9. Reconnecting with Family

With his heart lighter and his spirit renewed, James made an effort to reconnect with his family. He reached out to his mother, Mary, and apologized for the times he had pushed her away. Mary embraced him, her eyes filled with tears of joy.

"James, I've always believed in you," she said softly. "I'm so proud of the steps you're taking to heal and forgive. God has great plans for you, and I'm here to support you every step of the way."

James also reconnected with his siblings, who welcomed him with open arms. They spent time together, sharing stories, laughter, and the love that had always been there but had been overshadowed by James's struggles. The bonds of family were strengthened, and James felt a renewed sense of belonging.

10. Healing Through Service

Inspired by his own journey of forgiveness, James felt a calling to help others who were struggling with similar challenges. He began volunteering at the church, assisting with outreach programs and support groups focused on healing and reconciliation.

One of the most impactful initiatives James participated in was a program for individuals dealing with anger and resentment. He shared his own story of forgiveness, offering empathy and encouragement to those facing their own battles. His authenticity and vulnerability resonated deeply, providing hope and inspiration.

James also collaborated with Pastor David to create workshops and seminars on the power of forgiveness. These sessions provided a space for participants to explore their emotions, share their experiences, and find strength in their faith. The teachings of Ephesians 4:32 were at the heart of these programs, emphasizing kindness, compassion, and forgiveness.

11. Building a Supportive Community

As James became more involved in the church and community, he realized the importance of building a supportive network. He found joy in connecting with others, forming friendships based on trust, empathy, and shared faith.

The church community became a second family for James. They celebrated his successes, supported him in his struggles, and offered a constant source of encouragement. Through these connections, James experienced the transformative power of compassion and kindness.

James also organized support groups for those dealing with grief and loss. He understood that forgiveness was often intertwined with these experiences, and he wanted to provide a space for healing and growth. The support groups became a lifeline for many, offering a sense of hope and community.

12. Embracing a New Beginning

James's journey of forgiveness was transformative, not only for himself but for those around him. He had learned to let go of the past, to release the burdens of anger and resentment, and to embrace a new beginning. His faith had been a guiding force, providing strength and inspiration.

As he reflected on his journey, James felt a deep sense of gratitude for the people who had supported him, the lessons he had learned, and the grace of God that had carried him through. He knew that forgiveness was an ongoing process, but he was committed to living a life defined by kindness, compassion, and faith.

James's relationships with his family, friends, and colleagues had been transformed. The walls of bitterness that had once isolated him were replaced by connections built on trust and empathy. He found joy in the small moments, in the love and laughter that filled his life.

13. A Testament of Faith

One Sunday, Pastor David invited James to share his testimony during a church service. Standing before the congregation, James felt a mixture of nervousness and gratitude. He knew that his story could offer hope and encouragement to others who were struggling with forgiveness.

"Forgiveness is not easy," James began, his voice steady. "But it is a gift we give ourselves. It frees us from the burden of resentment and allows us to experience the grace and love of God. Ephesians 4:32 reminds us to be kind and compassionate, forgiving each other just as Christ forgave us. I have learned that forgiveness is a journey, and through faith, we can find peace and freedom."

James shared his experiences, the challenges he had faced, and the transformative power of forgiveness. His authenticity and vulnerability resonated deeply with the congregation, offering a message of hope and healing.

After the service, many members of the congregation approached James, expressing their gratitude for his testimony. They shared their own struggles with forgiveness and found comfort in knowing that they were not alone. James felt a profound sense of purpose, knowing that his journey had made a difference in the lives of others.

14. Continuing the Journey

James knew that his journey of forgiveness was ongoing. There would be new challenges and opportunities for growth, but he faced the future with confidence, trusting in God's presence and guidance. His faith had become the cornerstone of his life, providing strength and inspiration.

He continued to be involved in the church, offering support and guidance to those in need. His work with the anger and grief support groups was particularly fulfilling, as he witnessed the healing and transformation that came from forgiveness and faith.

James also pursued personal growth, seeking to deepen his understanding of forgiveness and compassion. He attended workshops, read books on spiritual growth, and sought mentorship from Pastor David. Through these efforts, he continued to grow in his faith and his ability to offer empathy and support to others.

15. Embracing the Power of Forgiveness

As James reflected on his journey, he felt a deep sense of gratitude for the people who had supported him, the lessons he had learned, and the grace of God that had carried him through. He knew that forgiveness was an ongoing process, but he was committed to living a life defined by kindness, compassion, and faith.

James's relationships with his family, friends, and colleagues had been transformed. The walls of bitterness that had once isolated him were replaced by connections built on trust and empathy. He found joy in the small moments, in the love and laughter that filled his life.

One evening, as James knelt in prayer, he thanked God for the journey of forgiveness he had undertaken. He reflected on the ways his faith had grown, the healing he had experienced, and the peace that now filled his heart. He knew that the power of forgiveness had not only changed his life but had also allowed him to be a source of light and hope for others.

Conclusion

"The Power of Forgiveness" in "Streams of Hope: An Anthology of Faith" tells the story of James Thompson, a man who learns to forgive those who wronged him, discovering freedom and peace through his faith. Guided by the words of Ephesians 4:32, his journey illustrates the transformative power of forgiveness and the grace of God.

James's transformation from a place of bitterness and resentment to one of peace and compassion is a testament to the presence of God and the power of His love. His story serves as a beacon of hope and inspiration, reminding us all that, no matter the challenges we face, we can find strength and joy in forgiveness and faith.

Through his journey, James discovers the importance of faith, community, and compassion. His testimony offers encouragement and support to those facing their own battles, illustrating the truth that forgiveness is a gift we give ourselves, and through it, we can experience the grace and love of God.

Chapter 10: Streams in the Desert

Bible Verse: Isaiah 35:6 - "Then will the lame leap like a deer, and the mute tongue shout for joy. Water will gush forth in the wilderness and streams in the desert."

1. The Call to Serve

Sarah Williams had always felt a calling to serve others. From a young age, she was drawn to missionary work, inspired by the stories of her parents who had spent years in Africa as medical missionaries. After completing her theological studies, Sarah joined a missionary organization and was assigned to a remote, drought-stricken region in East Africa.

The region, known as Kijiji, had been suffering from severe drought for several years. The lack of water had devastating effects on the community, leading to crop failure, livestock deaths, and a severe scarcity of drinking water. The people of Kijiji were resilient, but the continuous struggle for survival took its toll on their spirits.

Sarah's mission was to provide not only spiritual guidance but also practical support. She was determined to help the people of Kijiji find hope and strength in their faith while working towards solutions to the challenges they faced. Her journey was one of faith, service, and the belief that miracles could happen even in the most desperate circumstances.

2. The Arrival in Kijiji

Sarah arrived in Kijiji with a mixture of excitement and apprehension. The landscape was stark and arid, a stark contrast to the lush greenery she was used to back home. The villagers greeted her warmly, their smiles a testament to their enduring hope despite the hardships they faced.

She quickly set to work, partnering with local leaders to understand the community's needs and priorities. The lack of water was the most pressing issue, affecting every aspect of life in Kijiji. Sarah knew that finding a sustainable water source was critical to the community's survival and well-being.

She also focused on building relationships, earning the trust of the villagers through her compassion and dedication. Sarah held prayer meetings, offered counseling, and provided educational support to the children. Her presence brought a sense of hope and renewal, reminding the villagers that they were not alone in their struggles.

3. The Challenge of Water

The search for water in Kijiji was a daunting task. The region's dry climate and rocky terrain made traditional methods of finding water difficult. Wells dug in the past had run dry, and attempts to bring water from distant sources had failed due to logistical challenges and lack of resources.

Sarah reached out to her missionary organization and other aid groups, seeking expertise and support for the project. Engineers and hydrologists were brought in to assess the situation and explore potential solutions. The initial reports were discouraging, but Sarah's faith and determination remained unshaken.

She organized community meetings to discuss the water crisis, involving villagers in brainstorming and planning sessions. The sense of unity and collective effort was palpable, as everyone understood the critical importance of the mission. The villagers' faith was a source of strength, and they prayed fervently for a solution.

4. The Power of Prayer

Throughout the process, prayer became a cornerstone of Sarah's work in Kijiji. She led prayer meetings, where villagers gathered to seek God's guidance and intervention. They prayed for rain, for wisdom in finding water, and for the strength to persevere.

One evening, during a particularly moving prayer session, Sarah shared the verse from Isaiah 35:6: "Then will the lame leap like a deer, and the mute tongue shout for joy. Water will gush forth in the wilderness and streams in the desert."

The words resonated deeply with the villagers, offering a promise of hope and renewal.

The power of prayer was evident in the community's resilience and unity. Despite the challenges, their faith remained strong, and they continued to support one another. Sarah found inspiration in their unwavering belief, knowing that their collective faith could move mountains.

5. The Miraculous Discovery

After months of searching and countless setbacks, a breakthrough occurred. A team of hydrologists discovered an underground aquifer beneath a rocky outcrop on the outskirts of Kijiji. The water was deep and required significant effort to access, but it was a promising source that could potentially transform the community.

The news spread quickly, filling the villagers with renewed hope and excitement. Sarah organized a meeting to discuss the next steps, involving local leaders, engineers, and volunteers. The task ahead was formidable, requiring drilling equipment, manpower, and coordination.

Despite the challenges, the community rallied together with determination and faith. Fundraising efforts were launched, and resources were pooled. Sarah's missionary organization provided additional support, and neighboring communities offered their assistance. The sense of unity and purpose was inspiring.

6. The Drilling Begins

The day the drilling equipment arrived in Kijiji was a momentous occasion. Villagers gathered to witness the start of the project, their hearts filled with hope and anticipation. The drilling process was arduous and slow, requiring careful planning and execution.

Sarah and the villagers continued to pray, seeking God's guidance and protection throughout the process. They understood that the journey was not just about finding water but also about strengthening their faith and trust in God's provision.

As the drilling progressed, the community faced several setbacks. Equipment failures, unexpected rock formations, and technical challenges tested their resolve. But each time, they came together in prayer, drawing strength from their faith and each other.

7. The Breakthrough

After weeks of relentless effort, the moment they had all been praying for arrived. The drilling team hit water, and a powerful stream gushed forth from the ground. The sight was nothing short of miraculous, and the villagers erupted in cheers and tears of joy.

Sarah led the community in a prayer of thanksgiving, their voices filled with gratitude and praise. The words of Isaiah 35:6 echoed in their hearts, a testament to the fulfillment of God's promise. The water was not just a physical necessity but a symbol of hope, renewal, and divine provision.

The aquifer provided a sustainable source of clean water, transforming the lives of the villagers. Crops flourished, livestock thrived, and the daily struggle for water became a thing of the past. The miracle of water in the desert strengthened the faith of the entire community, reminding them of God's enduring love and care.

8. Building a New Future

With the newfound water source, Kijiji embarked on a journey of renewal and growth. Sarah worked with local leaders to implement sustainable agricultural practices, ensuring that the community could make the most of their resources. Irrigation systems were set up, and new crops were introduced, enhancing food security and economic stability.

The availability of clean water also improved the villagers' health and well-being. The incidence of waterborne diseases decreased, and children could attend school regularly without the burden of fetching water. The community's overall quality of life improved, and a sense of optimism and possibility took root.

Sarah continued her mission, focusing on education and spiritual growth. She established a school, providing children with access to quality education and nurturing their potential. The school became a beacon of hope, inspiring the next generation to dream big and work towards a brighter future.

9. Strengthening Faith

The miraculous provision of water had a profound impact on the community's faith. The villagers' belief in God's love and provision was strengthened, and their trust in His plans deepened. The verse from Isaiah 35:6 became a cornerstone of their faith, a reminder of the miracles that faith and prayer could bring.

Sarah continued to lead prayer meetings and Bible study groups, helping the villagers grow in their spiritual journey. The teachings of the Bible provided guidance, comfort, and inspiration, reinforcing the values of compassion, unity, and resilience.

The church in Kijiji became a vibrant center of worship and community life. Services were filled with joyous singing, heartfelt prayers, and testimonies of God's goodness. The sense of community and shared faith was palpable, creating a strong foundation for the village's future.

10. The Role of Service

Sarah's mission in Kijiji was not just about providing physical resources but also about fostering a spirit of service and compassion. She encouraged the villagers to support one another, to extend kindness and help to those in need, and to work together for the common good.

Service became a way of life in Kijiji, with villagers volunteering their time and skills to support various community projects. They built homes for those in need, provided care for the elderly, and supported local businesses. The spirit of service and generosity strengthened the bonds within the community and created a culture of mutual support.

Sarah also emphasized the importance of looking beyond their village to help others. The villagers organized outreach programs to support neighboring communities facing similar challenges. Their experiences and successes inspired others, creating a ripple effect of hope and transformation.

11. Personal Growth and Transformation

Sarah's journey in Kijiji was transformative not only for the community but also for herself. She experienced personal growth and deepened her own faith, witnessing firsthand the power of prayer, the strength of community, and the miracles that God could bring.

Her time in Kijiji taught her valuable lessons about resilience, compassion, and the importance of faith in the face of adversity. She developed a deeper understanding of the interconnectedness of physical and spiritual well-being and the ways in which faith could inspire and sustain communities.

Sarah also built lasting relationships with the villagers, forming deep bonds of friendship and mutual respect. The love and gratitude she received from the community were profoundly rewarding, reaffirming her calling to serve and her belief in the power of faith and compassion.

12. Sharing the Story

The story of Kijiji's transformation spread beyond the village, inspiring many others. Sarah documented the journey, sharing the experiences, challenges, and miracles that had defined their path. Her accounts were published in missionary newsletters, church bulletins, and online platforms, reaching a wide audience.

The story of Kijiji became a testament to the power of faith, prayer, and community. It illustrated the profound impact that compassion, unity, and

divine intervention could have on transforming lives and creating lasting change. The story also inspired other missionary efforts, encouraging people to believe in the possibility of miracles and the importance of serving others.

Sarah was invited to speak at various churches and conferences, sharing the story of Kijiji and the lessons learned. Her testimony resonated deeply with audiences, offering hope and encouragement to those facing their own challenges. The words of Isaiah 35:6 became a beacon of inspiration, reminding people of God's promise to bring streams in the desert and joy in the wilderness.

13. The Ongoing Mission

The journey in Kijiji was far from over. The community continued to grow and evolve, building on the foundation of faith, resilience, and service. Sarah remained committed to her mission, supporting the villagers in their ongoing efforts to create a sustainable and thriving community.

New projects and initiatives were launched, focusing on education, healthcare, and economic development. The school expanded, offering more opportunities for children and young adults to pursue their dreams. Healthcare services were improved, with a focus on preventive care and community health education.

The spirit of service and compassion continued to define the community, with villagers taking on leadership roles and driving positive change. The bonds of friendship and faith that had been forged through the trials and triumphs created a strong and enduring foundation for the future.

14. A Testament of Faith

Kijiji's journey from drought-stricken despair to a thriving, hopeful community was a testament to the power of faith and the promise of Isaiah 35:6. The villagers' belief in God's provision, their resilience in the face of adversity, and their commitment to supporting one another created a story of transformation and renewal.

Sarah often reflected on the journey, feeling a deep sense of gratitude for the opportunity to serve and witness the miracles that faith could bring. She knew that the true strength of Kijiji lay in the hearts and spirits of its people, and she was inspired by their unwavering faith and determination.

The story of Kijiji became a beacon of hope and inspiration for many, illustrating the profound impact that faith, community, and compassion could have on transforming lives and creating lasting change. The words of Isaiah 35:6 remained a constant reminder of God's promise and the miracles that faith could bring.

15. Looking to the Future

As Sarah and the villagers of Kijiji looked to the future, they embraced a vision of continued growth, resilience, and compassion. The journey from drought to abundance had taught them valuable lessons about the power of faith, the strength of community, and the importance of service.

They remained committed to building a sustainable and thriving community, driven by the values of kindness, unity, and faith. New projects and initiatives were planned, focusing on education, healthcare, and economic development. The spirit of service and compassion continued to define their efforts, creating a culture of mutual support and empowerment.

The church remained a central hub of community life, providing spiritual guidance, support, and a space for connection. Services were filled with joyous singing, heartfelt prayers, and testimonies of God's goodness. The sense of community and shared faith was palpable, creating a strong foundation for the village's future.

Sarah's mission in Kijiji was ongoing, and she felt a deep sense of purpose and fulfillment in her work. She knew that the journey was far from over, but she faced the future with confidence, trusting in God's presence and guidance. The words of Isaiah 35:6 remained a beacon of inspiration, reminding her of the miracles that faith and prayer could bring.

Conclusion

"Streams in the Desert" in "Streams of Hope: An Anthology of Faith" tells the story of Sarah Williams, a missionary who witnesses a miraculous provision of water in a drought-stricken region. Guided by the words of Isaiah 35:6, her journey illustrates the transformative power of faith, prayer, and community.

The transformation of Kijiji from a place of despair to a thriving, hopeful community is a testament to the presence of God and the power of His love. The story serves as a beacon of hope and inspiration, reminding us all that, no matter the challenges we face, we can find strength and joy in God's promises.

Through her journey, Sarah discovers the importance of faith, service, and compassion. Her testimony offers encouragement and support to those facing their own battles, illustrating the truth that God's promise of streams in the desert and joy in the wilderness will prevail, even in the darkest of times.

Chapter 11: Hope Restored

Bible Verse: Romans 15:13 - "May the God of hope fill you with all joy and peace as you trust in him, so that you may overflow with hope by the power of the Holy Spirit."

1. The Unexpected Blow

David Martin was a man who prided himself on his work ethic. As a mid-level manager at a large corporation, he had spent the better part of two decades climbing the corporate ladder. He was respected by his colleagues, admired for his dedication, and considered his career a cornerstone of his identity. That was until the fateful day when everything changed.

David had sensed the winds of change blowing through the company. Rumors of restructuring and layoffs were rampant, but he had never imagined he would be among those affected. He had poured his heart and soul into his job, often working long hours and sacrificing personal time to ensure the success of his team and the company.

The news came in the form of a brief meeting with his supervisor and an HR representative. The company was downsizing, and David's position was being eliminated. The words felt like a punch to the gut. He left the office with a severance package and a head full of questions about his future.

2. The Aftermath

The days following his layoff were a blur of confusion and despair. David found himself waking up early, his body still accustomed to his old routine, only to remember that he no longer had a job to go to. The structure and purpose that his career had provided were suddenly gone, leaving a void that seemed impossible to fill.

David's wife, Lisa, was a pillar of support during this difficult time. She encouraged him to take some time to process his emotions and assured him that they would get through this together. Despite her reassurances, David felt an overwhelming sense of failure. He struggled with feelings of inadequacy and fear about their financial stability.

The severance package provided temporary relief, but David knew it wouldn't last forever. He spent hours each day updating his resume, searching for job openings, and submitting applications. Despite his best efforts, weeks turned into months with no promising leads. The constant rejection took a toll on his self-esteem, and he began to question his worth and purpose.

3. A Crisis of Faith

David had always considered himself a man of faith. He attended church regularly, prayed, and believed in the teachings of the Bible. But in the wake of his job loss, he found himself grappling with doubts and questions. Why had this happened to him? What was God's plan in all of this? He felt abandoned and struggled to maintain his faith in the face of such uncertainty.

Lisa noticed the changes in her husband. She saw the weight of his burden and the way it was affecting his spirit. She gently encouraged him to turn to God in prayer, reminding him of the verse from Romans 15:13: "May the God of hope fill you with all joy and peace as you trust in him, so that you may overflow with hope by the power of the Holy Spirit."

David was skeptical at first. He felt distant from God and wasn't sure if prayer would make a difference. But one sleepless night, in the quiet of their living room, he decided to give it a try. He knelt and poured out his heart to God, sharing his fears, frustrations, and doubts. It was a raw and honest prayer, filled with vulnerability and longing.

4. Finding Comfort in Prayer

To his surprise, David felt a sense of peace wash over him as he prayed. It wasn't an immediate solution to his problems, but it was a comforting presence that reassured him he wasn't alone. He began to pray regularly, finding solace in the act of turning his burdens over to God.

Prayer became a lifeline for David. Each morning, he started his day with a quiet moment of reflection and prayer, seeking guidance and strength. He read the Bible more frequently, finding inspiration and comfort in the scriptures.

Romans 15:13 became a guiding light, reminding him to trust in God and to find hope and peace in His presence.

Lisa joined David in his spiritual journey. They prayed together, attended church services, and participated in Bible study groups. Their shared faith became a source of strength for their marriage, helping them navigate the challenges they faced together.

5. A New Perspective

As David's faith grew, so did his perspective on his situation. He began to see his job loss not as a failure, but as an opportunity for growth and transformation. He realized that his identity and worth were not tied to his career, but to his faith and the values he held dear.

David started to explore new interests and passions. He volunteered at their church, helping with community outreach programs and offering support to others who were facing difficult times. He found fulfillment in serving others, discovering a sense of purpose that went beyond his professional achievements.

Through his volunteer work, David connected with people from all walks of life. He heard their stories of struggle and resilience, and he shared his own journey of faith and hope. These interactions reminded him of the importance of compassion, empathy, and the power of community.

6. An Unexpected Opportunity

One day, while volunteering at a local food bank, David struck up a conversation with another volunteer, Mark. Mark was a retired businessman who had started his own consulting firm. He was impressed by David's dedication and work ethic and asked him about his professional background.

David shared his story, including the challenges he had faced since losing his job. Mark listened intently and offered some valuable advice. He suggested that David consider leveraging his skills and experience to start his own consulting business. It was an idea that had never crossed David's mind, but the more they talked, the more it seemed like a viable option.

Mark offered to mentor David, providing guidance on how to start and grow a consulting business. He introduced him to potential clients and helped him navigate the complexities of entrepreneurship. With Mark's support and Lisa's encouragement, David took the leap and started his own consulting firm.

7. Building a New Future

Starting his own business was both exhilarating and daunting. David faced a steep learning curve, but his faith and determination kept him moving forward. He drew on his years of experience, leveraging his skills to provide valuable services to his clients. Slowly but surely, his business began to grow.

David found joy and fulfillment in his new venture. He enjoyed the challenge of building something from the ground up and the freedom to set his own direction. He also appreciated the opportunity to help other businesses succeed, knowing that his work made a positive impact.

Throughout this journey, David's faith remained a guiding force. He continued to pray and seek God's guidance, trusting that he was on the right path. Romans 15:13 served as a constant reminder to trust in God and to find hope and peace in His presence.

8. Strengthening Relationships

As David's business grew, so did his relationships with his family and community. He made a conscious effort to balance his work with quality time spent with Lisa and their children. They went on family outings, shared meals, and created lasting memories together.

David also reconnected with friends and colleagues, building a network of support and collaboration. He valued the relationships he had built over the years and was grateful for the people who had stood by him during his darkest times.

His involvement in the church deepened, as he took on leadership roles and helped organize community events. He found joy in serving others and in being part of a supportive and compassionate community. His faith was not just a private practice but a living, breathing part of his daily life.

9. Overcoming Challenges

Despite the progress he had made, David faced challenges along the way. Running a business was not without its difficulties, and there were times when he felt overwhelmed and uncertain. But his faith and the support of his loved ones helped him navigate these obstacles.

When faced with difficult decisions, David turned to prayer, seeking God's wisdom and guidance. He trusted that God had a plan for him and that each challenge was an opportunity for growth. His faith provided a sense of peace and assurance, even in the face of uncertainty.

Lisa remained his steadfast partner, offering encouragement and support. Together, they faced the ups and downs of life, knowing that their faith and love for each other would carry them through. Their marriage grew stronger, built on a foundation of trust, respect, and shared values.

10. A Newfound Purpose

David's journey of faith and resilience led him to discover a newfound purpose. He realized that his experience of losing his job and finding a new direction had equipped him to help others facing similar challenges. He felt a calling to share his story and to offer support and encouragement to those in need.

He began speaking at church events, community gatherings, and business seminars, sharing his journey of faith, hope, and entrepreneurship. His story resonated with many, offering a message of hope and inspiration. He emphasized the importance of trusting in God, finding joy and peace in His presence, and being open to new opportunities.

David also started a support group for individuals who had lost their jobs or were facing career transitions. The group provided a safe space for people to share their experiences, offer encouragement, and explore new possibilities. It became a source of community and empowerment, reminding members that they were not alone in their struggles.

11. A Testimony of Faith

One Sunday, David was invited to share his testimony during a church service. Standing before the congregation, he felt a deep sense of gratitude and humility. He knew that his journey was a testament to the power of faith and the grace of God.

"Brothers and sisters," David began, "I stand before you today, not as a man who has all the answers, but as someone who has experienced the transformative power of faith and the love of God. When I lost my job, I felt like my world had crumbled. I was filled with fear, doubt, and a sense of failure."

He paused, looking out at the faces of the congregation. "But it was through prayer and trust in God that I found hope and a new direction. Romans 15:13 reminds us to trust in God, to be filled with joy and peace, and to overflow with hope by the power of the Holy Spirit. This verse became my guiding light, helping me navigate the darkest moments and find a path forward."

David shared the journey of starting his own business, the challenges he faced, and the support he received from his family and community. He spoke about the importance of service, compassion, and the strength that comes from faith.

"My friends," he concluded, "no matter what challenges you face, know that God is with you. Trust in Him, and He will guide you. Find joy and peace in His presence, and let His love fill your heart. Together, we can overcome any obstacle and find hope and purpose in His plan."

The congregation responded with heartfelt applause, moved by David's testimony. His story of resilience and faith resonated deeply, offering encouragement and inspiration to all who heard it.

12. Continuing the Journey

David knew that his journey of faith and entrepreneurship was ongoing. There would be new challenges and opportunities for growth, but he faced the future with confidence, trusting in God's presence and guidance. His faith had become the cornerstone of his life, providing strength and inspiration.

He continued to be involved in the church and community, offering support and guidance to those in need. His work with the support group and his speaking engagements were particularly fulfilling, as he witnessed the healing and transformation that came from faith and community.

David also pursued personal growth, seeking to deepen his understanding of faith, leadership, and entrepreneurship. He attended workshops, read books on spiritual growth and business, and sought mentorship from experienced leaders. Through these efforts, he continued to grow in his faith and his ability to offer empathy and support to others.

13. Embracing the Power of Hope

As David reflected on his journey, he felt a deep sense of gratitude for the people who had supported him, the lessons he had learned, and the grace of God that had carried him through. He knew that hope was a powerful force, capable of transforming lives and creating lasting change.

He embraced the power of hope, finding joy and peace in God's presence. He understood that hope was not just a fleeting feeling but a deep and abiding trust in God's promises. Romans 15:13 remained a guiding verse, reminding him to trust in God and to find strength and joy in His love.

David's relationships with his family, friends, and colleagues had been transformed. The struggles he had faced had strengthened his bonds with those he loved, and he found joy in the small moments, in the love and laughter that filled his life.

14. A Community Transformed

David's journey had a ripple effect on the community around him. His story of resilience and faith inspired many, encouraging others to trust in God and to find hope in difficult times. The support group he started became a thriving community, offering encouragement and empowerment to its members.

The church community also grew stronger, with a renewed focus on compassion, service, and faith. David's testimony and leadership helped to create a culture of support and collaboration, reminding everyone of the importance of trusting in God and helping one another.

The businesses that David worked with through his consulting firm also benefited from his guidance and support. He helped them navigate challenges, find new opportunities, and build strong, resilient organizations. His work made a positive impact, creating a ripple effect of growth and success.

15. Looking to the Future

As David looked to the future, he embraced a vision of continued growth, resilience, and service. The journey from job loss to entrepreneurship had taught him valuable lessons about the power of faith, the strength of community, and the importance of hope.

He remained committed to building a sustainable and thriving business, driven by the values of integrity, compassion, and excellence. New projects and initiatives were planned, focusing on innovation, collaboration, and community engagement. The spirit of service and generosity continued to define his efforts, creating a culture of mutual support and empowerment.

The church remained a central hub of community life, providing spiritual guidance, support, and a space for connection. Services were filled with joyous singing, heartfelt prayers, and testimonies of God's goodness. The sense of community and shared faith was palpable, creating a strong foundation for the future.

David's mission was ongoing, and he felt a deep sense of purpose and fulfillment in his work. He knew that the journey was far from over, but he faced the future with confidence, trusting in God's presence and guidance. The words of Romans 15:13 remained a beacon of inspiration, reminding him of the hope, joy, and peace that come from trusting in God.

Conclusion

"Hope Restored" in "Streams of Hope: An Anthology of Faith" tells the story of David Martin, a man who finds hope and a new direction in life through prayer and trust in God after losing his job. Guided by the words of Romans 15:13, his journey illustrates the transformative power of faith, hope, and community.

David's transformation from a place of despair to one of hope and purpose is a testament to the presence of God and the power of His love. His story serves as a beacon of hope and inspiration, reminding us all that, no matter the challenges we face, we can find strength and joy in God's promises.

Through his journey, David discovers the importance of faith, service, and compassion. His testimony offers encouragement and support to those facing their own battles, illustrating the truth that hope is a powerful force, capable of transforming lives and creating lasting change.

Chapter 12: A New Song

Bible Verse: Psalm 40:3 - "He put a new song in my mouth, a hymn of praise to our God. Many will see and fear the Lord and put their trust in him."

1. A Lost Melody

Nathan Reed had once been a rising star in the world of music. A prodigy with a guitar, his talent was undeniable, and his passion for music was matched only by his drive to succeed. Nathan's journey from a small-town boy to a renowned musician was marked by hard work, dedication, and a series of fortunate breaks. However, the pressures of the music industry, combined with personal struggles, eventually led him to lose his way.

Nathan's career took off in his early twenties. His soulful voice and masterful guitar skills quickly gained him a following. He signed with a major record label, released successful albums, and embarked on nationwide tours. Yet, the very success he had dreamed of brought with it unexpected challenges. The constant pressure to perform, the endless travel, and the demand for new material took a toll on his mental and physical health.

As Nathan's career progressed, he found himself increasingly isolated. The relationships he had cherished became strained, and the joy he once found in music began to fade. He turned to alcohol and drugs to cope with the stress and loneliness, leading to a downward spiral that ultimately resulted in the collapse of his career. His label dropped him, and he retreated from the public eye, feeling like a failure.

2. Hitting Rock Bottom

The years that followed were some of the darkest in Nathan's life. He struggled with addiction, depression, and a deep sense of purposelessness. The guitar that had once been an extension of his soul now sat untouched in a corner of his apartment. The music that had filled his life with meaning and joy seemed like a distant memory.

Nathan's family and friends tried to reach out, but he pushed them away, ashamed of his fall from grace. He moved back to his hometown, hoping to find some semblance of peace, but the familiar surroundings only reminded him of what he had lost. The community that had once celebrated his success now seemed to look at him with pity and disappointment.

One night, after a particularly heavy bout of drinking, Nathan found himself alone in his apartment, staring at the bottle in his hand. He felt a profound sense of emptiness, a void that nothing seemed to fill. In that moment of despair, he cried out to God, something he hadn't done in years. "God, if you're there, I need help. I can't do this on my own anymore."

3. The First Steps to Healing

Nathan's cry for help marked the beginning of a new journey. The next morning, he woke up with a sense of clarity he hadn't felt in a long time. He knew he needed to make a change, and that change had to start with his relationship with God. Nathan's faith had been a significant part of his upbringing, but he had drifted away from it during his pursuit of fame.

He reached out to Pastor John, the minister at the church he had attended as a child. Pastor John remembered Nathan well and welcomed him with open arms. They sat down for a long conversation, where Nathan poured out his heart, sharing his struggles and his desire to find a new path.

Pastor John listened with compassion and understanding. He reminded Nathan of the story of the prodigal son, who, after losing everything, returned home to find his father waiting with open arms. "God is always ready to welcome us back, Nathan," Pastor John said gently. "He can help you find a new song, a new purpose for your life."

With Pastor John's support, Nathan began attending church regularly. He also started seeing a counselor to address his addiction and mental health issues. These first steps were challenging, but they marked the beginning of Nathan's journey towards healing and restoration.

4. Rediscovering Music

As Nathan worked on his recovery, he found himself drawn back to music. Pastor John encouraged him to pick up his guitar again, suggesting that music could be a therapeutic outlet. At first, Nathan was hesitant. The guitar represented a time in his life filled with pain and regret. But as he began to play again, he found that music had the power to heal as well as hurt.

Nathan started by playing simple hymns and worship songs, finding comfort in their familiar melodies and uplifting messages. Gradually, he began to compose his own music again. This time, his songs were different. They were filled with raw emotion and a deep sense of spirituality. Music became a way for Nathan to process his journey, to express his faith, and to connect with God.

One Sunday, Pastor John asked Nathan if he would consider playing a song during the church service. Nathan was nervous, but he agreed. As he stood before the congregation, guitar in hand, he felt a mixture of fear and hope. He closed his eyes and began to play, singing a song he had written about finding hope in the midst of despair.

The response from the congregation was overwhelming. People were moved by Nathan's music, and many approached him after the service to share how his song had touched their hearts. For Nathan, this experience was a powerful affirmation that he was on the right path. It rekindled his love for music and his desire to use his gift to serve God and others.

5. A New Direction

With his faith and passion for music restored, Nathan began to explore new opportunities. He felt called to use his talents to make a positive impact, and he started by volunteering at local community centers and schools. He taught music lessons, organized concerts, and shared his story with young people who were facing their own challenges.

Nathan's journey of rediscovery also led him to reconnect with his family and friends. He reached out to those he had pushed away, seeking forgiveness and rebuilding relationships. His loved ones were supportive and encouraged by the changes they saw in him. Their love and acceptance provided a strong foundation for Nathan's continued growth.

Inspired by Psalm 40:3, "He put a new song in my mouth, a hymn of praise to our God. Many will see and fear the Lord and put their trust in him," Nathan felt compelled to write new music that reflected his faith journey. His songs were filled with messages of hope, redemption, and the power of God's love. He began to perform at local churches, events, and even small venues, sharing his testimony through his music.

6. Building a Ministry

As Nathan's music ministry grew, he felt a calling to do more. He wanted to reach a wider audience and to provide a platform for other artists who shared his vision. With the support of Pastor John and his church, Nathan founded a non-profit organization called "New Song Ministries."

The mission of New Song Ministries was to inspire and uplift through music, providing opportunities for musicians to share their gifts and their faith. The organization hosted concerts, workshops, and outreach programs, bringing music and hope to communities in need. Nathan's journey from despair to purpose became the cornerstone of the ministry's message.

Nathan also began collaborating with other Christian artists, creating music that blended different styles and cultures. These collaborations enriched his work and expanded the ministry's reach. He found joy in the creative process and in the relationships he built with fellow musicians.

7. Overcoming Challenges

The path of rebuilding his life and ministry was not without challenges. Nathan faced moments of doubt and insecurity, questioning whether he was truly capable of making a difference. There were times when the old temptations of addiction and despair resurfaced, threatening to derail his progress.

In these moments, Nathan relied on his faith and the support of his community. He continued to pray, read scripture, and seek guidance from Pastor John and his counselor. The verse from Psalm 40:3 served as a constant reminder of God's faithfulness and the new song He had placed in Nathan's heart.

Nathan also found strength in the stories of others who had overcome adversity. He listened to testimonies of faith and resilience, drawing inspiration from their journeys. These stories reinforced his belief that God could use even the darkest moments for good, transforming pain into purpose.

8. Making an Impact

New Song Ministries quickly gained momentum, touching the lives of many through its programs and events. Nathan's story of redemption and faith resonated with audiences, offering hope and encouragement. His music became a powerful tool for ministry, breaking down barriers and connecting people to the message of God's love.

One of the most impactful initiatives was a series of music workshops for at-risk youth. Nathan and his team provided music lessons, mentorship, and opportunities for performance. The workshops gave young people a sense of purpose and belonging, helping them to build confidence and express themselves creatively.

Nathan also organized benefit concerts to raise funds for various causes, such as disaster relief, poverty alleviation, and mental health support. These events brought communities together and demonstrated the power of music to inspire change. Nathan's leadership and passion inspired others to get involved, creating a ripple effect of positive impact.

9. Personal Growth and Reflection

Throughout his journey, Nathan experienced significant personal growth. He developed a deeper understanding of his faith and his purpose, and he learned valuable lessons about resilience, humility, and compassion. His relationship with God became the foundation of his life, guiding his decisions and actions.

Nathan also reflected on the importance of authenticity in his music and ministry. He realized that his struggles and failures were an integral part of his story, and that sharing them openly could help others who were facing similar challenges. His willingness to be vulnerable and honest created a powerful connection with his audience.

As he looked back on his journey, Nathan felt a deep sense of gratitude for the people who had supported him, the lessons he had learned, and the ways in which God had worked in his life. He knew that his story was a testament to the power of faith and the transformative potential of God's love.

10. Expanding the Vision

As New Song Ministries continued to grow, Nathan felt a calling to expand its reach even further. He envisioned a network of music ministries that could collaborate and support one another, amplifying their impact and bringing hope to more communities.

To achieve this vision, Nathan launched the "New Song Network," a coalition of music ministries, artists, and organizations dedicated to using music for ministry and social change. The network provided resources, training, and opportunities for collaboration, fostering a sense of community and shared purpose.

The New Song Network quickly gained traction, attracting members from across the country and beyond. Nathan traveled extensively, meeting with fellow musicians and ministry leaders, sharing his vision, and building partnerships. The network's influence grew, and its impact was felt in churches, schools, and communities around the world.

11. A Testimony of Faith

One Sunday, Nathan was invited to share his testimony during a church service. Standing before the congregation, he felt a deep sense of gratitude and humility. He knew that his journey was a testament to the power of faith and the grace of God.

"Friends," Nathan began, "I stand before you today as someone who has experienced the highs and lows of life. I once lost my way, consumed by the pressures of success and the darkness of addiction. But through God's grace and the support of my loved ones, I found my way back to faith and to the music that fills my soul."

He paused, looking out at the faces of the congregation. "Psalm 40:3 says, 'He put a new song in my mouth, a hymn of praise to our God. Many will see and fear the Lord and put their trust in him.' This verse has been a guiding light for me, reminding me that God's love can transform even the darkest moments into something beautiful."

Nathan shared his journey of rediscovery, the challenges he faced, and the ways in which his faith had been restored. He spoke about the power of music to heal and inspire, and the importance of using one's gifts to serve others.

"My friends," he concluded, "no matter what challenges you face, know that God is with you. Trust in Him, and He will guide you. Let Him put a new song in your heart, and use that song to bring hope and joy to the world."

The congregation responded with heartfelt applause, moved by Nathan's testimony. His story of resilience and faith resonated deeply, offering encouragement and inspiration to all who heard it.

12. Continuing the Journey

Nathan knew that his journey of faith and music was ongoing. There would be new challenges and opportunities for growth, but he faced the future with confidence, trusting in God's presence and guidance. His faith had become the cornerstone of his life, providing strength and inspiration.

He continued to be involved in New Song Ministries and the New Song Network, offering support and guidance to fellow musicians and ministry leaders. His work with at-risk youth and community outreach programs was particularly fulfilling, as he witnessed the healing and transformation that music could bring.

Nathan also pursued personal growth, seeking to deepen his understanding of faith, leadership, and creativity. He attended workshops, read books on spiritual growth and music, and sought mentorship from experienced leaders. Through these efforts, he continued to grow in his faith and his ability to offer empathy and support to others.

13. Embracing the Power of Music

As Nathan reflected on his journey, he felt a deep sense of gratitude for the people who had supported him, the lessons he had learned, and the grace of God that had carried him through. He knew that music was a powerful force, capable of transforming lives and creating lasting change.

He embraced the power of music, finding joy and fulfillment in using his gifts to serve God and others. He understood that music was not just a profession but a calling, a way to connect with people and to share the message of God's love.

Nathan's relationships with his family, friends, and colleagues had been transformed. The struggles he had faced had strengthened his bonds with those he loved, and he found joy in the small moments, in the love and laughter that filled his life.

14. A Community Transformed

Nathan's journey had a ripple effect on the community around him. His story of redemption and faith inspired many, encouraging others to trust in God and to find hope in difficult times. The work of New Song Ministries and the New Song Network brought people together, fostering a sense of community and shared purpose.

The church community also grew stronger, with a renewed focus on compassion, service, and faith. Nathan's testimony and leadership helped to create a culture of support and collaboration, reminding everyone of the importance of trusting in God and helping one another.

The musicians and artists who worked with Nathan were inspired by his vision and passion. They found joy and fulfillment in their creative work, knowing that their music could make a positive impact. Together, they created a vibrant and dynamic community, united by their faith and their love for music.

15. Looking to the Future

As Nathan looked to the future, he embraced a vision of continued growth, resilience, and service. The journey from despair to purpose had taught him valuable lessons about the power of faith, the strength of community, and the importance of music.

He remained committed to building a sustainable and thriving ministry, driven by the values of integrity, compassion, and excellence. New projects and initiatives were planned, focusing on innovation, collaboration, and community engagement. The spirit of service and generosity continued to define his efforts, creating a culture of mutual support and empowerment.

The church remained a central hub of community life, providing spiritual guidance, support, and a space for connection. Services were filled with joyous singing, heartfelt prayers, and testimonies of God's goodness. The sense of community and shared faith was palpable, creating a strong foundation for the future.

Nathan's mission was ongoing, and he felt a deep sense of purpose and fulfillment in his work. He knew that the journey was far from over, but he faced the future with confidence, trusting in God's presence and guidance. The words of Psalm 40:3 remained a beacon of inspiration, reminding him of the new song God had placed in his heart and the ways in which his music could bring hope and joy to the world.

Conclusion

"A New Song" in "Streams of Hope: An Anthology of Faith" tells the story of Nathan Reed, a talented musician who rediscovers his gift and purpose through his faith. Guided by the words of Psalm 40:3, his journey illustrates the transformative power of music, faith, and community.

Nathan's transformation from a place of despair to one of hope and purpose is a testament to the presence of God and the power of His love. His story serves as a beacon of hope and inspiration, reminding us all that, no matter the challenges we face, we can find strength and joy in God's promises.

Through his journey, Nathan discovers the importance of faith, service, and compassion. His testimony offers encouragement and support to those facing their own battles, illustrating the truth that God can put a new song in our hearts, filling us with hope and guiding us to use our gifts for His glory.

Chapter 13: The Gift of Love

Bible Verse: 1 Corinthians 13:13 - "And now these three remain: faith, hope and love. But the greatest of these is love."

1. The Loss

Margaret Sullivan had always believed that she and her husband, Thomas, would grow old together. They had met in college, fallen in love, and built a life filled with laughter, adventure, and a deep sense of partnership. Their bond was strong, rooted in shared faith and mutual respect. But life, with its unpredictable twists and turns, had different plans.

Thomas had been diagnosed with a rare and aggressive form of cancer. Despite their best efforts and the support of doctors, family, and friends, Thomas passed away within a year of his diagnosis. Margaret was devastated. The man who had been her rock, her confidant, and her best friend was gone, leaving behind a void that seemed impossible to fill.

In the weeks following Thomas's death, Margaret struggled to navigate her grief. Every corner of their home reminded her of him, and the pain of his absence was overwhelming. She found it difficult to sleep, eat, or find any semblance of normalcy. Friends and family tried to console her, but their words often felt hollow. Margaret's faith, which had been a source of strength throughout her life, now seemed distant and elusive.

2. A Time of Mourning

Margaret's days were filled with a profound sense of loss. She would often sit in Thomas's favorite chair, holding a photo album of their memories together. Tears flowed freely as she reminisced about their life, from their wedding day to the countless small moments that had defined their relationship.

The community rallied around her, offering support and comfort. Her church family was particularly present, providing meals, praying with her, and offering a shoulder to cry on. Pastor Elizabeth, a close friend of Margaret's, spent many evenings sitting with her, listening and offering words of solace.

"Margaret, it's okay to mourn," Pastor Elizabeth said gently one evening. "Grief is a journey, and it's different for everyone. But remember, you are not alone. God is with you, and so are we. 1 Corinthians 13:13 reminds us that faith, hope, and love remain, and the greatest of these is love. Thomas's love for you, and your love for him, will always be a part of you."

Margaret appreciated the support, but she still felt lost. She prayed, asking God for strength and guidance, but her prayers often felt like they were falling into a void. She questioned why this had happened and struggled to find meaning in her pain.

3. The Glimmer of Hope

One particularly difficult night, Margaret found herself unable to sleep. She went to her living room, sat in Thomas's chair, and opened her Bible. It fell open to 1 Corinthians 13, and her eyes settled on verse 13: "And now these three remain: faith, hope and love. But the greatest of these is love."

As she read the verse, a sense of peace washed over her. She realized that, even in the midst of her grief, love remained. The love she and Thomas had shared was still a part of her, and it always would be. That love, she realized, was a gift from God, a testament to His presence in their lives.

Margaret began to see her grief in a new light. Instead of being consumed by the pain of loss, she started to focus on the love that continued to exist. She understood that love was a powerful force, capable of transcending even death. This realization was a turning point, giving her a glimmer of hope and a renewed sense of faith.

4. Rebuilding Faith

With this newfound perspective, Margaret made a conscious effort to reconnect with her faith. She attended church regularly, participated in Bible study groups, and spent time in prayer. The scriptures, particularly those about love and hope, became a source of comfort and strength.

Pastor Elizabeth and other church members supported Margaret in her journey. They encouraged her to share her feelings and to lean on her faith community. Margaret found that, as she opened up about her grief, she felt less alone. Others shared their own stories of loss and healing, creating a bond of shared experience and mutual support.

Margaret also began to volunteer at her church, finding solace in service. She helped with various activities, from organizing events to providing support to those in need. This sense of purpose gave her a reason to get out of bed each day and helped her to slowly rebuild her life.

5. A New Purpose

One day, while volunteering at a church event, Margaret met another widow named Sarah. Sarah had recently lost her husband and was struggling with the same feelings of grief and isolation that Margaret had experienced. They struck up a conversation, and Margaret shared her journey of faith and healing.

Sarah was deeply moved by Margaret's story. She found comfort in knowing that she was not alone and that healing was possible. Margaret realized that her experiences could be a source of hope for others. She felt a calling to help those who were going through similar situations, to offer them the same support and love that she had received.

Inspired by this realization, Margaret approached Pastor Elizabeth with an idea. She wanted to start a support group for widows and widowers, a place where they could come together to share their stories, support one another, and find healing through faith. Pastor Elizabeth was enthusiastic about the idea and offered her full support.

6. The Healing Hearts Group

The support group, named Healing Hearts, held its first meeting a few weeks later. Margaret was nervous but hopeful. She had prepared a short introduction, sharing her story and the Bible verse that had given her so much comfort: 1 Corinthians 13:13.

The response was overwhelmingly positive. The group members, each with their own unique stories of loss, found solace in the shared experience. They prayed together, read scriptures, and offered words of encouragement. The sense of community and mutual support was palpable, creating a safe space for healing and growth.

As the weeks went by, the Healing Hearts group grew in size and strength. Margaret facilitated the meetings, guiding discussions and ensuring that everyone felt heard and supported. She also organized guest speakers, including grief counselors and pastors, who provided additional insights and resources.

The group members found comfort in the regular meetings, knowing that they had a place to go where they could share their feelings without judgment. They formed deep bonds, supporting one another through the ups and downs of the grieving process. Margaret was amazed at the transformation she saw in herself and in others, as they moved from a place of pain to one of healing and hope.

7. Spreading the Message

The success of the Healing Hearts group inspired Margaret to do more. She felt a calling to share her message of hope and love with a wider audience. With Pastor Elizabeth's encouragement, she began speaking at other churches and community events, sharing her story and the impact of the support group.

Margaret's testimony resonated deeply with many. Her honesty about her struggles and her faith journey offered a beacon of hope to those who were facing their own losses. She emphasized the importance of community, faith, and love, and how these elements had helped her to find healing.

She also wrote a series of articles for the church newsletter, sharing practical advice and spiritual insights for those dealing with grief. Her writings reached a wide audience, offering comfort and encouragement to readers both within and beyond her church community.

8. The Power of Love

Throughout her journey, Margaret discovered the profound power of love. She realized that love was not just an emotion but a force that could bring healing and transformation. The love she had shared with Thomas continued to live on, inspiring her to reach out to others and to offer them the gift of love.

Margaret's understanding of love deepened as she read and reflected on the scriptures. 1 Corinthians 13 became a foundational text for her, particularly verse 13: "And now these three remain: faith, hope and love. But the greatest of these is love." She saw how love was the thread that connected faith and hope, creating a tapestry of resilience and strength.

She also experienced the love of her community in profound ways. The support and encouragement she received from her church family were tangible expressions of God's love. This sense of belonging and connection reinforced her belief in the importance of love as a cornerstone of faith.

9. Embracing New Opportunities

As Margaret continued to heal and grow, new opportunities emerged. She was invited to participate in a church conference on grief and healing, where she shared her story and led a workshop on building support groups. The conference provided a platform for Margaret to connect with others who were passionate about helping those in need.

Margaret also began to collaborate with local organizations that provided support to widows and widowers. She offered her expertise in creating and facilitating support groups, helping these organizations to expand their reach and impact. Her work was recognized and appreciated, and she found joy in knowing that she was making a difference.

One of the most fulfilling opportunities came when Margaret was invited to co-author a book on grief and faith. The book, titled "The Gift of Love: Finding Hope in the Midst of Loss," combined personal stories, practical advice, and spiritual reflections. Writing the book was a cathartic experience for Margaret, allowing her to articulate her journey and to share the lessons she had learned.

10. A Testimony of Faith

One Sunday, Pastor Elizabeth invited Margaret to share her testimony during a church service. Standing before the congregation, Margaret felt a deep sense of gratitude and humility. She knew that her journey was a testament to the power of faith, hope, and love.

"Friends," Margaret began, "I stand before you today as someone who has experienced profound loss and found healing through the grace of God. When I lost my husband, Thomas, I was consumed by grief and despair. But through the support of my faith community and the love of God, I found a new purpose and a renewed sense of hope."

She paused, looking out at the faces of the congregation. "1 Corinthians 13:13 says, 'And now these three remain: faith, hope and love. But the greatest of these is love.' This verse has been a guiding light for me, reminding me that love is the foundation of our faith and the source of our strength."

Margaret shared her journey of healing, the challenges she faced, and the ways in which her faith had been restored. She spoke about the power of community and the importance of supporting one another in times of need.

"My friends," she concluded, "no matter what challenges you face, know that you are not alone. God is with you, and His love surrounds you. Trust in Him, and He will guide you. Let love be your foundation, and you will find the strength to overcome any obstacle."

The congregation responded with heartfelt applause, moved by Margaret's testimony. Her story of resilience and faith resonated deeply, offering encouragement and inspiration to all who heard it.

11. Continuing the Journey

Margaret knew that her journey of faith and healing was ongoing. There would be new challenges and opportunities for growth, but she faced the future with confidence, trusting in God's presence and guidance. Her faith had become the cornerstone of her life, providing strength and inspiration.

She continued to be involved in the Healing Hearts group and other support initiatives, offering guidance and encouragement to those in need. Her work with widows and widowers was particularly fulfilling, as she witnessed the healing and transformation that came from community and faith.

Margaret also pursued personal growth, seeking to deepen her understanding of faith, love, and service. She attended workshops, read books on spiritual growth and grief support, and sought mentorship from experienced leaders. Through these efforts, she continued to grow in her faith and her ability to offer empathy and support to others.

12. Embracing the Power of Love

As Margaret reflected on her journey, she felt a deep sense of gratitude for the people who had supported her, the lessons she had learned, and the grace of God that had carried her through. She knew that love was a powerful force, capable of transforming lives and creating lasting change.

She embraced the power of love, finding joy and fulfillment in using her experiences to serve God and others. She understood that love was not just an emotion but a calling, a way to connect with people and to share the message of God's grace.

Margaret's relationships with her family, friends, and church community had been transformed. The struggles she had faced had strengthened her bonds with those she loved, and she found joy in the small moments, in the love and laughter that filled her life.

13. A Community Transformed

Margaret's journey had a ripple effect on the community around her. Her story of resilience and faith inspired many, encouraging others to trust in God and to find hope in difficult times. The Healing Hearts group and other support initiatives brought people together, fostering a sense of community and shared purpose.

The church community also grew stronger, with a renewed focus on compassion, service, and faith. Margaret's testimony and leadership helped to create a culture of support and collaboration, reminding everyone of the importance of trusting in God and helping one another.

The widows and widowers who participated in the support group found healing and hope, knowing that they were not alone in their grief. The bonds they formed and the love they shared created a strong and resilient community, united by their faith and their experiences.

14. Looking to the Future

As Margaret looked to the future, she embraced a vision of continued growth, resilience, and service. The journey from grief to hope had taught her valuable lessons about the power of faith, the strength of community, and the importance of love.

She remained committed to building a sustainable and thriving ministry, driven by the values of integrity, compassion, and excellence. New projects and initiatives were planned, focusing on innovation, collaboration, and community engagement. The spirit of service and generosity continued to define her efforts, creating a culture of mutual support and empowerment.

The church remained a central hub of community life, providing spiritual guidance, support, and a space for connection. Services were filled with joyous singing, heartfelt prayers, and testimonies of God's goodness. The sense of community and shared faith was palpable, creating a strong foundation for the future.

Margaret's mission was ongoing, and she felt a deep sense of purpose and fulfillment in her work. She knew that the journey was far from over, but she faced the future with confidence, trusting in God's presence and guidance. The words of 1 Corinthians 13:13 remained a beacon of inspiration, reminding her of the enduring power of faith, hope, and love.

Conclusion

"The Gift of Love" in "Streams of Hope: An Anthology of Faith" tells the story of Margaret Sullivan, a widow who finds comfort and hope in her faith after the loss of her spouse. Guided by the words of 1 Corinthians 13:13, her journey illustrates the transformative power of love, faith, and community.

Margaret's transformation from a place of grief to one of hope and purpose is a testament to the presence of God and the power of His love. Her story serves as a beacon of hope and inspiration, reminding us all that, no matter the challenges we face, we can find strength and joy in God's promises.

Through her journey, Margaret discovers the importance of faith, service, and compassion. Her testimony offers encouragement and support to those facing their own battles, illustrating the truth that love is a powerful force, capable of transforming lives and creating lasting change.

Chapter 14: Courageous Faith

Bible Verse: Joshua 1:9 - "Have I not commanded you? Be strong and courageous. Do not be afraid; do not be discouraged, for the Lord your God will be with you wherever you go."

1. The Challenge

Alex Carter was a typical high school junior navigating the complexities of adolescence. He was an honor student, played on the soccer team, and had a close-knit group of friends. But there was one aspect of Alex's life that set him apart: his unwavering faith. Raised in a devout Christian family, Alex's beliefs were deeply ingrained in his identity. However, high school was a challenging environment for expressing his faith openly.

In a secular public school, Alex often found himself in situations where his beliefs were questioned or even ridiculed. Despite this, he had always managed to maintain a low profile, practicing his faith quietly and avoiding confrontation. But everything changed when the school decided to implement a new policy prohibiting religious symbols and expressions on campus.

The new policy sparked outrage among many students and parents, but it was particularly challenging for Alex. Wearing a small cross necklace had always been a silent but significant way for him to express his faith. When he was asked to remove it, Alex felt a deep sense of conflict. Should he comply and avoid trouble, or should he stand up for his beliefs?

2. A Moment of Decision

The night after the policy was announced, Alex sat at the dinner table with his parents, John and Mary Carter, discussing the situation. John, a deacon at their church, and Mary, a Sunday school teacher, were both proud of Alex's faith but also concerned about the potential repercussions of defying the school policy.

"Alex, you know we support you no matter what," John said gently. "But you need to think carefully about how you want to handle this. Standing up for your beliefs can be difficult and may come with consequences."

Mary nodded in agreement. "Remember Joshua 1:9, Alex. 'Be strong and courageous. Do not be afraid; do not be discouraged, for the Lord your God will be with you wherever you go.' We will pray for you and trust that God will guide you in making the right decision."

That night, Alex prayed fervently for wisdom and courage. He thought about the example he wanted to set, not just for himself, but for his younger siblings and friends. He knew that standing up for his faith was the right thing to do, even if it meant facing challenges and opposition.

3. Taking a Stand

The next morning, Alex walked into school with a sense of determination. He wore his cross necklace visibly, ready to face whatever came his way. As he entered the building, he noticed the curious and sometimes disapproving looks from his peers and teachers. He felt a knot of anxiety in his stomach but reminded himself of Joshua 1:9 and the promise that God would be with him.

By lunchtime, the word had spread that Alex was defying the new policy. Some students admired his bravery, while others saw it as an act of rebellion. Alex's closest friends gathered around him, offering their support. They knew how important his faith was to him and respected his decision.

During his third-period class, the principal, Mr. Jenkins, called Alex to his office. As Alex walked through the hallways, he could feel the weight of the moment. He prayed silently for strength and guidance, knowing that this meeting could determine the course of his high school experience.

4. The Principal's Office

Mr. Jenkins greeted Alex with a stern but concerned expression. "Alex, I understand that you're wearing a cross necklace despite the new policy. Can you explain why you're choosing to defy the rules?"

Alex took a deep breath and met the principal's gaze. "Mr. Jenkins, my cross necklace is more than just a piece of jewelry. It's a symbol of my faith and a reminder of who I am and what I believe in. I respect the school's authority, but I also believe that I have the right to express my faith openly."

Mr. Jenkins listened intently, his expression softening slightly. "I understand that this is important to you, Alex. However, the policy was put in place to maintain a neutral environment for all students. We don't want anyone to feel excluded or uncomfortable because of religious differences."

Alex nodded. "I understand the intention behind the policy, but I believe that respecting each other's beliefs is part of what makes our school a diverse and inclusive place. By allowing students to express their faith, we're promoting tolerance and understanding, not division."

Mr. Jenkins sighed, leaning back in his chair. "I see your point, Alex. This is a difficult situation, and I need to consider the implications carefully. I'll discuss this with the school board and let you know their decision. In the meantime, I ask that you respect the policy during school hours."

Alex felt a mix of relief and uncertainty as he left the office. He had spoken his truth, but the outcome was still uncertain. He continued to wear his cross necklace, waiting for the final decision from the school board.

5. The School Board Meeting

The news of Alex's stand quickly spread, sparking discussions among students, parents, and faculty. Some supported Alex's right to express his faith, while others argued that the policy should be upheld to maintain neutrality. The school board scheduled a special meeting to address the issue, inviting input from the community.

On the day of the meeting, the school auditorium was packed with students, parents, and community members. Alex and his family sat near the front, feeling the weight of the moment. Mr. Jenkins opened the meeting, explaining the reasons behind the policy and the situation with Alex.

Several parents and students spoke, sharing their perspectives on the issue. Some emphasized the importance of respecting individual beliefs, while others voiced concerns about maintaining a neutral environment. The debate was heated, but Alex remained calm, praying for wisdom and courage.

When it was Alex's turn to speak, he stood at the podium, feeling the eyes of the entire room on him. He took a deep breath and began. "Thank you for allowing me to speak. I understand the school's intention to create a neutral environment, but I believe that true inclusivity means respecting and allowing the expression of all beliefs. My cross necklace is a symbol of my faith, and wearing it is an important part of who I am."

He paused, looking out at the audience. "Joshua 1:9 says, 'Be strong and courageous. Do not be afraid; do not be discouraged, for the Lord your God will be with you wherever you go.' I believe that standing up for my faith is part of being courageous. I hope that we can find a way to respect each other's beliefs and create a truly inclusive environment."

The room was silent for a moment before a wave of applause erupted. Alex returned to his seat, feeling a sense of relief and accomplishment. The school board members conferred and eventually announced their decision: the policy would be revised to allow students to wear religious symbols, as long as they were respectful and did not disrupt the learning environment.

6. Inspiring Others

Alex's stand for his beliefs had a ripple effect throughout the school. His courage inspired other students to express their faith openly, whether through wearing religious symbols or participating in faith-based clubs and activities. The atmosphere of the school began to shift, becoming more inclusive and accepting of diverse beliefs.

Alex's actions also sparked important conversations about faith, tolerance, and respect. Teachers and students discussed these topics in classrooms, fostering a deeper understanding of the importance of respecting individual beliefs. The school's administration implemented new programs to promote diversity and inclusivity, ensuring that all students felt valued and respected.

One of the most significant outcomes was the formation of an interfaith club, where students of different religious backgrounds could come together to share their beliefs and learn from one another. Alex played a key role in founding the club, working with students, teachers, and community leaders to create a space for open dialogue and mutual respect.

7. Personal Growth

Through his experience, Alex grew in ways he had never anticipated. He developed a deeper understanding of his faith and a stronger sense of purpose.

He realized that being a Christian wasn't just about attending church or reading the Bible but about living out his beliefs with integrity and courage.

Alex also discovered the power of community and the importance of standing together. His friends, family, and church had supported him throughout the ordeal, providing encouragement and strength. He learned that he didn't have to face challenges alone and that faith was stronger when shared with others.

The experience also strengthened Alex's relationship with his family. John and Mary were proud of their son's courage and commitment to his faith. They continued to support him, encouraging him to use his experiences to inspire and help others.

8. A Newfound Purpose

With a renewed sense of purpose, Alex became more involved in his church and community. He volunteered for various outreach programs, participated in mission trips, and mentored younger students who were struggling with their faith. He saw his role as not just a student but a leader and an example for others to follow.

Alex's story spread beyond his school and community, reaching people through social media, local news, and church networks. He was invited to speak at youth conferences, church events, and community gatherings, sharing his testimony and encouraging others to stand up for their beliefs.

Each time he spoke, Alex emphasized the importance of Joshua 1:9 and the message of courage and faith. He shared how his experience had taught him to trust in God's presence and to be strong and courageous, no matter the challenges. His words resonated with many, offering hope and inspiration.

9. Challenges and Opportunities

While Alex's stand for his faith brought many positive changes, it also came with its share of challenges. There were still those who disagreed with his views and who felt that religious expressions should be kept private. Alex faced criticism and opposition, both online and in person.

However, these challenges only strengthened his resolve. Alex learned to handle criticism with grace and to engage in respectful dialogue with those who held different beliefs. He saw these interactions as opportunities to learn and grow, and to demonstrate the love and compassion that were central to his faith.

Alex also faced personal challenges, balancing his schoolwork, extracurricular activities, and his growing role as a faith leader. There were times when he felt overwhelmed and uncertain, but he continued to rely on his faith and the support of his community. He reminded himself of Joshua 1:9 and the promise that God would be with him wherever he went.

10. A Lasting Impact

As Alex approached his senior year, he reflected on the journey he had taken since that pivotal day when he decided to stand up for his faith. He saw how his actions had not only changed his own life but had also made a lasting impact on his school and community.

The interfaith club he had helped to found continued to thrive, fostering understanding and respect among students of different backgrounds. The school's new policies and programs promoted inclusivity and diversity, creating a more welcoming environment for all students.

Alex's leadership and courage had inspired many of his peers to embrace their own beliefs openly and to stand up for what they believed in. His story had reached beyond the walls of his school, touching the lives of countless people and encouraging them to live out their faith with courage and integrity.

11. Graduation and Beyond

As graduation approached, Alex felt a mix of excitement and nostalgia. He was proud of what he had accomplished and grateful for the support of his family, friends, and community. He looked forward to the future, knowing that his journey of faith was far from over.

On the day of his graduation, Alex was chosen to deliver the valedictory address. Standing before his classmates, teachers, and families, he felt a deep sense of gratitude and purpose. He shared his story once more, highlighting the importance of courage, faith, and community.

"Graduation is not just an end but a beginning," Alex said. "As we move forward, let us remember the lessons we've learned and the values we hold dear. Joshua 1:9 reminds us to be strong and courageous, to trust in God's presence, and to live out our faith with integrity. Let's carry these principles with us as we step into the next chapter of our lives."

The audience responded with a standing ovation, moved by Alex's words and the journey he had shared. As he looked out at the sea of faces, Alex felt a profound sense of fulfillment and hope.

12. Continuing the Mission

After graduation, Alex decided to attend a Christian college where he could further his education and deepen his faith. He chose to study theology and social work, with the goal of continuing to serve and inspire others. He saw his college years as an opportunity to grow, learn, and prepare for the future.

At college, Alex continued to be a leader and a role model. He joined campus ministries, led Bible study groups, and participated in service projects. He also continued to speak at various events, sharing his testimony and encouraging others to stand up for their beliefs.

Alex's experiences in college reinforced his commitment to living out his faith with courage and compassion. He formed deep friendships, learned from wise mentors, and discovered new ways to serve and inspire others. His journey of faith was a continuous process of growth and discovery.

13. Embracing the Future

As Alex approached the end of his college years, he felt a sense of anticipation and excitement for the future. He had grown in his faith, developed new skills, and formed a clear vision of how he wanted to serve God and his community.

He decided to pursue a career in ministry, feeling called to help others navigate their own faith journeys. He also wanted to continue his work with young people, providing support and guidance as they faced the challenges of adolescence and young adulthood.

Alex's family and friends supported his decision, encouraging him to follow his calling and to trust in God's plan. They were proud of the man he had become and the impact he had made on so many lives.

14. A Testament of Faith

One Sunday, Alex returned to his home church to share his journey with the congregation. Standing before the familiar faces of his church family, he felt a deep sense of gratitude and humility. He knew that his journey was a testament to the power of faith, courage, and community.

"Friends," Alex began, "I stand before you today as someone who has experienced the power of God's presence and the importance of standing up for what you believe in. When I faced challenges in high school, I learned to trust in Joshua 1:9: 'Have I not commanded you? Be strong and courageous. Do not be afraid; do not be discouraged, for the Lord your God will be with you wherever you go.'"

He paused, looking out at the congregation. "This verse has been a guiding light for me, reminding me to be courageous and to trust in God's presence. My journey has taught me that faith is not just a private belief but a way of living, a way of standing up for what is right and true."

Alex shared his experiences, the challenges he had faced, and the ways in which his faith had grown. He spoke about the importance of community and the power of love and support in navigating life's challenges.

"My friends," he concluded, "no matter what challenges you face, know that you are not alone. God is with you, and His love surrounds you. Be strong and courageous, and let your faith guide you. Together, we can make a difference and bring hope and light to the world."

The congregation responded with heartfelt applause, moved by Alex's testimony. His story of resilience and faith resonated deeply, offering encouragement and inspiration to all who heard it.

15. Looking to the Future

As Alex looked to the future, he embraced a vision of continued growth, resilience, and service. The journey from standing up for his faith in high school to becoming a leader in his community had taught him valuable lessons about the power of courage, faith, and community.

He remained committed to building a sustainable and thriving ministry, driven by the values of integrity, compassion, and excellence. New projects and initiatives were planned, focusing on innovation, collaboration, and community engagement. The spirit of service and generosity continued to define his efforts, creating a culture of mutual support and empowerment.

The church remained a central hub of community life, providing spiritual guidance, support, and a space for connection. Services were filled with joyous singing, heartfelt prayers, and testimonies of God's goodness. The sense of community and shared faith was palpable, creating a strong foundation for the future.

Alex's mission was ongoing, and he felt a deep sense of purpose and fulfillment in his work. He knew that the journey was far from over, but he faced the future with confidence, trusting in God's presence and guidance. The words of Joshua 1:9 remained a beacon of inspiration, reminding him of the importance of being strong and courageous, and of trusting in God's unwavering presence and love.

Conclusion

"Courageous Faith" in "Streams of Hope: An Anthology of Faith" tells the story of Alex Carter, a teenager who stands up for his beliefs at school and inspires others to embrace their faith openly. Guided by the words of Joshua 1:9, his journey illustrates the transformative power of courage, faith, and community.

Alex's transformation from a place of uncertainty to one of courage and purpose is a testament to the presence of God and the power of His love. His story serves as a beacon of hope and inspiration, reminding us all that, no matter the challenges we face, we can find strength and joy in God's promises.

Through his journey, Alex discovers the importance of faith, service, and compassion. His testimony offers encouragement and support to those facing their own battles, illustrating the truth that courage is a powerful force, capable of transforming lives and creating lasting change.

Chapter 15: Eternal Hope

Bible Verse: 2 Corinthians 4:16-18 - "Therefore we do not lose heart. Though outwardly we are wasting away, yet inwardly we are being renewed day by day. For our light and momentary troubles are achieving for us an eternal glory that far outweighs them all."

1. The Matriarch

Eleanor Martin had lived a full and blessed life. At eighty-seven years old, she was the matriarch of a large and loving family. Her life had been marked by faith, resilience, and an unwavering hope that had seen her through countless challenges and joys. Now, as she reflected on her journey, she felt a deep desire to share her wisdom and experiences with her grandchildren, hoping to instill in them the same sense of eternal hope that had sustained her.

Eleanor's home was a place of warmth and welcome. The walls were adorned with photographs chronicling the lives of her children and grandchildren, a testament to the love and legacy she had built. Her garden, meticulously tended, was a riot of color and life, a reflection of the beauty and abundance she saw in the world around her.

One sunny afternoon, as her grandchildren gathered for a family reunion, Eleanor decided it was the perfect time to share her story. She wanted them to understand the importance of faith and the eternal hope that had guided her through the many seasons of her life.

2. Gathering the Family

The family reunion was a lively affair, filled with laughter, stories, and the delicious aroma of home-cooked meals. Eleanor's children and grandchildren filled the house with energy and joy, their presence a reminder of the enduring bonds of family.

After the meal, Eleanor gathered her grandchildren in the living room. They ranged in age from toddlers to young adults, each one curious and eager to hear what their beloved grandmother had to share. Eleanor settled into her favorite armchair, a quilt she had made draped over her lap, and smiled at the eager faces before her.

"My dear grandchildren," she began, her voice warm and steady, "I want to share with you the story of my life and the lessons I've learned along the way. I hope that my journey will inspire you and give you strength as you face your own challenges. Remember the words of 2 Corinthians 4:16-18: 'Therefore we do not lose heart. Though outwardly we are wasting away, yet inwardly we are being renewed day by day. For our light and momentary troubles are achieving for us an eternal glory that far outweighs them all.'"

3. Early Years

Eleanor's story began in a small rural town where she was born and raised. Her family was devout, and faith was an integral part of their daily lives. She recounted her childhood with fondness, describing the simple joys of growing up surrounded by nature, family, and a close-knit community.

"My parents taught me the importance of faith from a young age," Eleanor said. "We attended church every Sunday, and our home was filled with prayer and Bible study. I learned to trust in God's plan, even when things were difficult. Those early lessons laid the foundation for my faith, which has sustained me throughout my life."

She spoke of the challenges her family faced during the Great Depression, a time of hardship and uncertainty. Yet, despite the difficulties, they never lost hope. Her parents' unwavering faith and resilience left a lasting impression on Eleanor, teaching her the value of perseverance and trust in God's provision.

4. Young Adulthood and Love

As Eleanor grew older, she faced new challenges and opportunities. She spoke of her decision to move to the city to pursue her education, a bold step for a young woman at the time. It was in the city that she met Samuel, the man who would become her husband and partner in life.

"Meeting Samuel was a blessing," Eleanor said, her eyes twinkling with the memory. "He was kind, hardworking, and shared my faith. Our courtship was filled with love, laughter, and a shared commitment to God. We married young and started our family, facing the joys and challenges of life together."

Eleanor recounted the early years of their marriage, the births of their children, and the ups and downs they experienced. She spoke of the importance of communication, mutual respect, and shared faith in building a strong and loving partnership.

"Samuel and I faced many challenges," she said, "but we always turned to God for guidance and strength. Our faith was the anchor that kept us grounded, and our love for each other grew stronger with each passing year."

5. Middle Years: Trials and Triumphs

Eleanor's life was not without its trials. She spoke candidly about the difficulties they faced, including financial struggles, health issues, and the loss of loved ones. Each challenge tested their faith, but they always found strength in their belief in God's eternal plan.

One of the most difficult periods in Eleanor's life was when Samuel was diagnosed with a serious illness. The news was devastating, and the road ahead was filled with uncertainty and fear. But through it all, Eleanor and Samuel remained steadfast in their faith, leaning on each other and their family for support.

"Those were some of the hardest days of my life," Eleanor said, her voice tinged with emotion. "But we never lost hope. We prayed together, trusted in God's plan, and found comfort in our faith. Samuel's strength and courage inspired me every day. Even in his final moments, he was at peace, knowing that he was going home to be with the Lord."

Eleanor paused, looking at her grandchildren. "Remember, my dear ones, that even in the darkest times, God's light is always with us. Our troubles are momentary, but the glory that awaits us is eternal."

6. The Later Years: Legacy and Wisdom

After Samuel's passing, Eleanor faced the challenge of navigating life without her beloved partner. It was a time of deep grief and reflection, but also of renewal and growth. She found solace in her faith and in the love of her family and friends.

"I realized that my journey was not over," Eleanor said. "I still had a purpose, and I wanted to honor Samuel's memory by living a life filled with love and faith. I became more involved in my church, volunteered in my community, and found joy in helping others."

Eleanor spoke of the importance of staying active and engaged, even in the later years of life. She encouraged her grandchildren to pursue their passions, to seek out opportunities to serve, and to always be open to learning and growth.

"Life is a precious gift," she said, "and each day is an opportunity to make a difference. Never stop seeking, never stop growing, and always hold on to your faith. It will guide you through every season of life."

7. Passing on the Legacy

As Eleanor shared her story, her grandchildren listened intently, their hearts touched by her words. They asked questions, seeking to understand more about her experiences and the lessons she had learned. Eleanor was grateful for their interest and eager to pass on the wisdom she had gained.

One of her granddaughters, Emily, asked, "Grandma, how do you stay so hopeful, even when things are hard?"

Eleanor smiled, her eyes reflecting the depth of her faith. "Hope is a gift from God, my dear. It is rooted in the belief that no matter what happens, God is with us and has a plan for our lives. Remember 2 Corinthians 4:16-18: 'Therefore we do not lose heart. Though outwardly we are wasting away, yet inwardly we are being renewed day by day. For our light and momentary troubles are achieving for us an eternal glory that far outweighs them all.'"

She continued, "When we focus on the eternal, rather than the temporary, we find strength and hope. Our faith renews us, and we can face any challenge with the confidence that God is with us. Hold on to that hope, and it will carry you through."

8. Stories of Faith and Hope

Eleanor shared more stories from her life, each one illustrating the power of faith and the importance of hope. She spoke of times when she had felt lost or uncertain, and how prayer and trust in God had guided her through.

One such story was about a particularly challenging time when the family business was struggling. "We were on the brink of losing everything," Eleanor recalled. "Samuel and I prayed fervently, seeking God's guidance. We didn't know how we would make it through, but we trusted that God had a plan."

Through hard work, perseverance, and the support of their community, they managed to turn things around. The experience taught Eleanor the value of resilience and the importance of relying on God's strength.

"Never underestimate the power of prayer and faith," she said. "When we surrender our worries to God and trust in His plan, we find the strength to overcome any obstacle."

9. The Importance of Community

Eleanor emphasized the importance of community and the role it had played in her life. She spoke of the support she had received from her church family, friends, and neighbors, especially during difficult times.

"Our community has been a source of strength and encouragement," she said. "We are not meant to walk this journey alone. Surround yourself with people who lift you up, who share your faith, and who will stand by you through thick and thin."

Eleanor encouraged her grandchildren to be active members of their communities, to build strong relationships, and to offer support to others. "Be there for one another," she said. "Love and support are powerful gifts that can make a world of difference."

10. The Gift of Love

As Eleanor's story drew to a close, she reflected on the central theme of her life: love. She spoke of the love she had shared with Samuel, the love she felt for her children and grandchildren, and the love of God that had been her constant companion.

"Love is the greatest gift we can give and receive," she said, her voice filled with emotion. "It is the foundation of our faith and the source of our hope. Remember 1 Corinthians 13:13: 'And now these three remain: faith, hope and love. But the greatest of these is love.'"

Eleanor's eyes filled with tears as she looked at her grandchildren. "I want you to know how much I love each of you and how proud I am of the people you are becoming. Carry that love with you, and let it guide your actions and decisions. Love one another, love yourselves, and above all, love God."

11. Embracing Eternal Hope

Eleanor's reflections on her life were a powerful testament to the enduring nature of faith, hope, and love. She wanted her grandchildren to understand that no matter what challenges they faced, they could always find strength and renewal in their faith.

"Life is full of ups and downs," she said, "but our faith is a constant source of strength. When we focus on the eternal, we can face any challenge with hope and courage. God's love is unfailing, and His promises are true. Hold on to that hope, and it will carry you through."

Eleanor's grandchildren were deeply moved by her words. They saw in her a living example of the power of faith and the beauty of a life well-lived. Her wisdom and love left a lasting impression, inspiring them to embrace their own journeys with courage and hope.

12. Passing the Torch

As the afternoon turned to evening, Eleanor's grandchildren hugged her tightly, expressing their gratitude for her stories and wisdom. They promised to carry her lessons with them and to live their lives with the same faith and hope that she had demonstrated.

Eleanor felt a deep sense of fulfillment. She knew that her legacy of faith, hope, and love would continue through her family. She had passed the torch, and she trusted that her grandchildren would carry it forward, lighting the way for future generations.

That night, as Eleanor lay in bed, she prayed a prayer of thanksgiving. She thanked God for the blessings of her life, for the love of her family, and for the eternal hope that had sustained her. She felt at peace, knowing that she had fulfilled her purpose and that her story would continue to inspire others.

13. A Family United

In the weeks and months that followed, Eleanor's family continued to draw strength and inspiration from her stories. They gathered more often, sharing meals, prayers, and moments of reflection. The bonds of love and faith that Eleanor had nurtured grew stronger, uniting the family in a shared sense of purpose and hope.

Eleanor's grandchildren carried her lessons into their own lives, finding strength in their faith and courage in the face of challenges. They pursued their dreams with confidence, knowing that their grandmother's legacy of hope and love was with them.

The family also became more involved in their community, following Eleanor's example of service and compassion. They volunteered at their church, supported local charities, and offered help to those in need. Eleanor's influence extended far beyond her immediate family, touching the lives of many in their community.

14. A Life Celebrated

As the years passed, Eleanor's health began to decline. She faced the challenges of aging with the same grace and faith that had defined her life. Her family surrounded her with love and support, cherishing every moment they had with her.

When Eleanor passed away peacefully in her sleep, her family mourned the loss of their beloved matriarch but celebrated the incredible life she had lived. Her funeral was a testament to her impact, attended by family, friends, and community members whose lives she had touched.

Pastor James, who had known Eleanor for many years, delivered the eulogy. He spoke of her unwavering faith, her boundless love, and the eternal hope that had guided her life. "Eleanor Martin was a beacon of light and hope," he said.

"She lived her life with courage and faith, and her legacy will continue to inspire us all."

15. Continuing the Legacy

Eleanor's family honored her memory by continuing the traditions and values she had instilled in them. They gathered regularly, shared their faith, and supported one another through life's challenges. They remembered her words of wisdom and the example she had set, finding strength and inspiration in her legacy.

Her grandchildren, now adults with families of their own, passed on Eleanor's teachings to their children. They shared stories of her life, read the Bible verses that had been so meaningful to her, and taught their children the importance of faith, hope, and love.

Eleanor's influence extended far beyond her family. The community she had served so faithfully continued to thrive, inspired by her example of compassion and service. Her story was told and retold, a testament to the power of a life lived with purpose and faith.

Conclusion

"Eternal Hope" in "Streams of Hope: An Anthology of Faith" tells the story of Eleanor Martin, an elderly woman who reflects on her life of faith and shares her wisdom and hope with her grandchildren. Guided by the words of 2 Corinthians 4:16-18, her journey illustrates the transformative power of faith, hope, and love.

Eleanor's life, filled with challenges and triumphs, is a testament to the enduring nature of God's promises. Her story serves as a beacon of hope and inspiration, reminding us all that, no matter the challenges we face, we can find strength and joy in God's eternal glory.

Through her journey, Eleanor discovers the importance of faith, service, and compassion. Her testimony offers encouragement and support to those facing their own battles, illustrating the truth that our light and momentary troubles are achieving for us an eternal glory that far outweighs them all.

Don't miss out!

Visit the website below and you can sign up to receive emails whenever Gregory Allen Parker publishes a new book. There's no charge and no obligation.

https://books2read.com/r/B-A-SLYZB-LTPCE

BOOKS 2 READ

Connecting independent readers to independent writers.

Did you love *Streams of Hope*? Then you should read *Voices of Faith*[1] by Gregory Allen Parker!

Voices of Faith: **Christian Short Stories** offers a collection of uplifting tales that explore the transformative power of faith. From a young girl's miracle in a village crisis to a pastor's inspiring dedication, each story highlights themes of hope, redemption, and compassion. Experience the profound impact of belief through miracles, personal trials, and acts of kindness, as diverse characters find strength and purpose in their faith. This anthology is a testament to the enduring power of prayer and the spirit of Christ's love in everyday life.

---

1. https://books2read.com/u/3G18Rr

2. https://books2read.com/u/3G18Rr

About the Author

Pastor Gregory Allen Parker, a graduate of Trinity Theological Seminary, is a devoted pastor and acclaimed author of Christian fiction. With over two decades of ministry experience, his books explore faith's challenges and triumphs, offering readers inspiring and spiritually rich narratives. Celebrated for his compassionate pastoral care and insightful sermons, Pastor Parker's storytelling reflects his deep understanding of Christian values. When not writing or preaching, he enjoys family time, community volunteering, and the outdoors, continuing to inspire and uplift through his faith and craft.